RING-RISE
RING-SET

MONICA HUGHES

RING-RISE RING-SET

A Magnet Book

Copyright © 1982 Monica Hughes
First published in Great Britain in 1982 by
Julia MacRae Books
A division of Franklin Watts Ltd
Magnet paperback edition first published 1983
by Methuen Children's Books Ltd
11 New Fetter Lane, London EC4P 4EE
Printed in Great Britain by
Richard Clay (The Chaucer Press) Ltd,
Bungay, Suffolk

ISBN 0 416 22930 1

Introduction

Thirty-four million years ago disaster struck Earth. The climate changed drastically. The giant mammals disappeared. What happened? The only clue lies in the presence of a great swathe of tectites lying across the surface of the Earth. Are these glassy particles the remnants of a meteor or a comet that came too close?

If this is what happened, the wreckage of this meteor would have formed a cloud of particles orbiting Earth. As Earth continued its diurnal spin, the particles would shrink back from the poles to form a huge ring around the equator, reaching perhaps from 4,000 to 12,000 miles into the sky, an opaque ring holding back the sun's energy from the temperate and polar latitudes of Earth. Each winter must have become colder, each year there would have been less vegetation.

The terminal Eocene event, if it happened that way, took place thirty-four million years ago. It *could* happen again...

1

It was a beautiful day, with the sun shining gold on the patch of ground between the two hydroponic tunnels; but in spite of the sun the women were covering the windows for winter.

If I were in charge, thought Liza, struggling with the heavy insulated shutter, I would leave everything open until the last possible moment before ringset. I would breathe every drop of fresh air I could, and catch every particle of sunshine.

She hammered the shutter with the flat of her hand. There. At last the wretched thing was cinched in place, the weather-proof gasket neatly overlapping the frame all round. She dropped the holding bar into its socket and clipped it tight.

At the next window she stopped to catch her breath. Through the frame she could see the view that lay beyond the outstretched arms of the tunnel greenhouses that extended southward from the City in the Hill. A patch of scrub willow outlined a small creek that was folded unexpectedly into the creases of the barren land. The leaves on the willows were brown and gold. They stirred gently. Out there the air must be alive and moving. As she pushed the next shutter into place she felt as if, in shutting out the sun and the moving leaves and the waters of the creek, she were denying life.

The big dining room grew dimmer as she put up each shutter. She had forgotten to turn on the overhead lights before she began. Typical Liza, her friends would say, never to look ahead. Now she felt as if she were slowly blinding the City. First one eye. Then the next. And the next. Until the room was dark. Was the sun still really shining outside?

In a few days the sun will be behind the ring. Winter will come and the ice will creep nearer, Liza thought. I'll be trapped inside the City for months and I can't bear it!

Without giving herself time to think of the consequences she ran out of the darkened room into the main hall. To her right was the Summer Door. It stood ajar, laying a small gold stripe of light along the floor. She looked quickly around. There was no one in sight, though she could hear the busy hum of the other women and girls readying the City for winter.

She crossed the stripe of gold and ran out into the sun, across the scrubby grass and down the slope to the willows along the creek. She ran fast, leaping over tussocks and stones, until she was safely hidden from view. She flung herself to the ground and lay gasping. The air was unexpectedly cold and it stung her throat. She rolled over onto her stomach and buried her face in the dry grass.

She could feel the sun on her shoulders, warming away the knots in her muscles that had come from handling the heavy shutters. Close to her ear the creek chattered softly. Liza listened to it intently, trying to find pattern and rhythm; but as soon as she thought she had discovered it, it would change. Putting her hand into the water changed the pattern too. The water grasped her hand, deathly cold. She bent over and drank from her cupped palms. It was so cold that it made her teeth ache, but it was sweet and living, not like the dead water in the City storage tanks. It tasted like the difference between a lit room and the sun shining outside.

Looking up from the creek she could see the northern sky, a huge empty bowl, glazed blue-green, clean and flawless. Not a cloud, not a bird. Nothing but a going on for ever. The land seemed to go on for ever too, a rolling tundra of dry grass and moss, dull green and brown and grey. At its end, below the horizon, was the great whiteness of the ice-sheet, every year a little closer. Its reflection glowed palely in the northern sky.

Closer was the curve of hillside that hid the City. Its four storeys of windows looked south, blankly shuttered. Liza knew no other home, and she hated it. It was like a prison.

She turned her back on it and looked south. Down there,

hundreds of miles below the tree-line, were real cities where it was still warm enough to go outdoors in winter. What must it be like, she wondered, to live in a house, just one family, to walk along streets and shop in real stores? To be free...

But Earth was at war with the ice, and Liza's father was one of the scientists at the front, battling the cold that crept relentlessly out of the north. He and Mother had lived in the City in the Hill since it was built. Liza had been born there. She had never been anywhere else in her whole life and she never would, unless the scientists succeeded in destroying the ring, or the ice won and forced them to move south.

She sighed and stared up at the ugly darkness of the ring, scrawled like a sooty archway across the southland, its shadow darkening Earth like the shadow of death. If you went far enough south, almost to the equator, the ring would be directly overhead, no thicker than a pencil line bisecting the sky. There would be no shadow. You would be warm all year round. Imagine...

Dry leaves rustled behind her and a hand clamped suddenly on her shoulder. She jumped and screamed. Then blushed when she saw who it was.

"Oh John, how you scared me!"

"What on earth are you doing out here? You'll catch it if you're found."

"You wouldn't tell?"

"What do you take me for? But how do you plan to get back inside without being noticed? Maybe you'd better come in with us. We've been fishing." He held up a string of Arctic char to prove his point. "But we're the last group out. Once we've checked in they'll probably lock the Summer Door. Look at the sun. Right on the edge of the ring. And you can feel the cold coming. It won't be long now."

"I know. We put up the shutters today. I don't want to come in with your crowd, John. Someone'll be sure to tell on me. Look, you could help me. Just check that the door's unlocked after the others have gone, that's all. *Please*."

3

"I'll have to take my fish to the kitchens first, you know. And suppose someone's in the hall when I get back? It's nearly dinner time. If someone saw me unlocking the door, then *I'd* get into trouble."

"Oh, John, don't make difficulties. It'll be easy."

"You're the one who's always making difficulties. Why do you *do* these things?"

"Oh, you'll never understand." Liza turned away and kicked at the stones edging the creek.

"Why don't you try me?" His voice was kind and unexpectedly warm. Liza felt a prickle of tears in her eyes. Usually people didn't talk to her like that. Usually their voices were waspish.

She blinked hard and turned to look at him. "You'd never understand. You don't know what it's like being a girl, stuck in the stupid City for ever and ever. It's so boring. At least you get to go fishing in summer and on scientific expeditions in winter. I'd give anything to be able to go out on an expedition..."

"You *want* to go outside after ringset?" John's voice went up. "You're crazy! Taking core samples and temperatures. To risk running into a horde of savage Ekoes. That's tough work, Liza. Man's work. You don't know when you're well off."

"Cooking? Cleaning? Keeping the City running? Huh!"

"Someone's got to do it." John swung his string of fish over his shoulder.

"But why us? What's so special about you men that you do all the interesting stuff and we have to do whatever you don't want?"

"It's the way life is, that's all. And you'd better start acting more like a girl or you'll get into real trouble."

"I don't care. And I hate you, John Watson. You're just like the others." She picked up a frozen clod and threw it at him, but he warded it off with one arm and walked away, arrogant, male.

Liza wanted to run after him, punch him in the ribs, smack

4

the string of fish across his stupid, smirking face. But then she heard the others coming. Their heavy feet pounded the ground as if they disliked it, and their loud voices drowned out the voice of the creek. She crouched in a patch of scrub willow until their voices faded into the distance.

The sound of the creek washed away her anger. She sighed and then shivered and looked up. It was getting very cold. The sun was low in the southwestern sky, its rim just touching the outer edge of the ring. The wind was strengthening, pouring heavy and cold down the slopes of the giant glaciers to the north. Her skin prickled under her light summer uniform. She'd die of exposure if she stayed out much longer!

She ran back to the City, stumbling on legs that were as rigid as frozen fish. The Summer Door was shut. She turned the knob. Shut and locked and barred. Bother! John had been right. She should have gone back with the others. Would he remember to come back and unlock it? Maybe he wouldn't want to. She shouldn't have chucked that lump of dirt at him. Why did she do things like that without thinking of the consequences?

"I don't care," she said aloud. "He was so maddening!"

She turned the knob again and pulled. Shook it. The door remained obstinately shut. Perhaps there was a window somewhere . . . she stepped back and looked up at the facade.

It stared blankly back at her, a wall of cement block set into the hillside, its four floors of windows blind and shut, lidded with winter shutters. There was nothing to break the monotony of the hundred and forty metre frontage, except for the plastic-covered tunnel greenhouses that ran forward like fat sausages from the east and west extremities of the building, and the sculptured shapes of the four solar traps and windmills that crested the hill.

It was blank and ugly and closed, and there was no way of getting back in without being noticed and punished, unless John forgave her and unlocked the Summer Door.

Away from the shelter of the hill Liza felt the full force of the north wind against her light tunic and trousers. She shivered and ran back to the door, her mind working frantically. High on the hillside to her right was the Winter Door, a triple-doored tunnel that plunged down through the inside of the hill to emerge in the underground storage area of the City. Perhaps...

She scrambled up the steep hillside. The wind howled and the sun set in an extravagance of crimson and gold. The Winter Door was shut.

Slowly the stars became visible. The cold was like a lump of ice in the pit of her stomach. A long shivering howl pierced the night and echoed to and fro among the low sad hills. Liza ran down the hill and hammered at the Summer Door with her fists, kicked at it with her sandalled feet.

It opened abruptly, catching her off balance so that she landed on all fours, down among the legs of the crowd that had gathered to discover the cause of the unusual racket. A large crowd, but absolutely silent. Liza looked up cautiously from among the feet, right into the cold grey eyes of Master Bix himself.

Now she'd really done it! She scrambled up and stood at attention in front of him, her eyes glued to the floor. She couldn't help noticing that the toes that protruded from his sandals were clean and well-shaped, the nails smooth and square. Her own feet, in contrast, were filthy, and her toes were swollen and an ugly purple colour, from the cold and door-kicking.

"So it's you again, Liza." The voice was resigned rather than angry, but Liza felt the lump inside her grow even colder and heavier. She shivered in spite of herself. "You're freezing, aren't you? Have a hot shower at once, and then take out your winter uniform from your chest. Be in my office in precisely fifteen minutes." He turned away. The crowd silently vanished. Liza was left alone.

Fifteen minutes! She bolted for the stairs, up two flights, along the corridor to the unit she shared with three other fifteen-year-olds. Breathlessly she kicked off her dusty sandals, dropped her uniform on the floor and grabbed a towel. It wasn't hers, but this was no time to be fussy.

The showers were at the end of the corridor, and at this time of the day they were completely deserted. If it wasn't for the threat of the visit to Master Bix's office hanging over her head she could have enjoyed a most luxurious shower. As it was she scrubbed her freezing body and washed the twigs and dead leaves out of her red hair with breathless haste.

Back in her room Liza scrambled desperately through her clothes chest for her winter uniform. I will tidy it up, she promised herself. If I get off this time I swear I'll never cause any trouble again. She tugged a comb – it was Win's, she couldn't find her own – through the wet tangle of hair. The tears sprang into her eyes at the pain, but she went on tugging ruthlessly until it lay, dark red and sleek, against her skull.

One minute left. Into the trousers. Then the tunic. Oh bother, back to front. Her arms waved wildly as she got it on right way round. Fresh sandals. Why did her spare pair have to have a broken strap? She remembered the day it had happened; she had honestly meant to take it straight down to the repair shop, only something else had happened and she'd forgotten. One of Letty's hair ribbons would hold it on for now. Only thirty seconds left ... she slammed out of the room and down the passage to the main corridor.

The supper warning-bell had just rung and the staircase was crowded with people coming upstairs to wash and tidy up after work. Every single person stared as if she were a visitor from Mars! Did everyone know that she had broken the rules again? Liza felt her cheeks grow red under the scrutiny of all those eyes. She dropped her gaze and sidled downstairs as close to the wall as she could get. Then she realised that she was the only person wearing winter uniform. No wonder she stuck out like an ink-blot on fresh paper! Every inhabitant of the City, from infant to grand-mother, was in summer blue, short-sleeved and loose-legged. Everyone except Liza Monroe. *She* looked like an over-ripe tomato in her orange-red winter suit, ribbed to fit at ankle and waist. She was a walking sign of what she was – someone who *had* to be different...

"But I don't mean to, honestly," she was saying ten minutes later. That was how long Master Bix's scolding had lasted. They were the first words she'd had a chance to say, and they weren't very clear, as her voice was still choked with tears. Not that Master Bix had said anything really *unkind*. Only being made to feel like a small worm of no account was, well, upsetting.

"Then why do you *do* these things?" Master Bix asked, in the calm tone of a man prepared to understand the explanation, however silly.

Liza gave a big sniff. Master Bix handed her a clean handkerchief just before she wiped her face on the sleeve of her clean winter uniform. She wiped her eyes and blew her nose while she thought about it.

"It's so boring being a girl," she discovered, and said so out loud.

Master Bix stared. "Boring? Don't you have sufficient work? Your timetable can be easily rearranged."

Enough to do? Didn't the chief know what it was like? Each month the women from one of the three dormitory floors were assigned to cook, clean, wash up, and do the laundry and mending for the six hundred inhabitants of the City. The senior woman, the floor Mother, doled out the jobs as she saw fit, ten women and girls to clean, twenty to cook, serve and wash up for six hundred hungry people thrice a day, forty more to do the laundry and mending.

It often seemed to Liza that the nastiest jobs went to the women that the floor Mother disliked or disapproved of; certainly it happened that every third month Liza faced a mound of pots and pans that never seemed to lessen from morning till night. Over and above that were the seasonal chores; putting up the winter shutters had been one of those.

The months that weren't filled with housework were devoted to school. Boring again, though she daren't say so to

Master Bix, who was the greatest brain in the City. And when she'd left school, what then? Liza sighed despairingly. A life of working in hydroponics or the yeast culture labs, producing the City's food, or seated at the looms where the fabric was woven, summer blue and winter red, for the uniforms everyone wore.

There was marriage, of course. Everyone married when they were about twenty, unless they were involved in a special study project and chose to postpone it. But what difference did marriage make anyway? You still went on doing the same dull work for the City. Even the babies were only looked after by their mothers for six months, and then the nursery took over. Parents were really much less important than Master Bix and one's own special floor Mother.

All this flashed through Liza's mind as she stood in front of Master Bix and tried to put her feelings into words. She scratched one foot against the other ankle, saw Master Bix stare at her feet, and remembered the broken sandal, mended with Letty's hair ribbon. She blushed and stopped fidgeting.

"Well? Don't you have enough to do? We've never had *that* complaint before." He was laughing at her, and she burst out with the first thing that came into her head.

"I wish I were a man. Men get to work on the really important things, like how to get rid of the ring and stop glaciers growing before they cover the whole world. That's exciting! They talk by radio to all the other men who are working on the ring, people from all over the world. They are allowed to go on expeditions outside. They're not stuck in the City for year after year the way we are. They can go fishing. At the very least girls ought to be allowed to go fishing!"

The corners of Master Bix's mouth twitched, but Liza didn't see. She was staring at the ground, mortified by her bad manners, but determined to go on now she had begun.

"I want to do something besides work in the kitchen. Something really useful." She dared to look up at his face again. "And exciting too," she added hastily, as he opened his mouth, surely to tell her how important eating was to the City, as if she didn't know.

"Did you have a special career in mind?" He sounded only mildly surprised by her outburst. "Tradition could be broken if you showed a special aptitude."

"Something scientific," Liza said vaguely. "To do with the ring."

"We need every new insight we can get," he answered surprisingly. "Perhaps we were wrong in excluding women from the professional work force . . . you must blame it on the pressure of the times . . . this need for a structured society has made us turn back to old-fashioned ideas. Perhaps we *should* make some changes. Give me your identity number, please."

She held out her right wrist and he typed into the computer the number on the bracelet. They waited in silence. The typewriter began to chatter and then spat out a length of paper. Master Bix tore it off and read it in silence. He looked at her, his eyebrows raised alarmingly, and read it again out loud.

"Mathematics 46. Physics 39. Biological Sciences 51. Shall I go on?"

"No, sir," Liza muttered, crimson up to her forehead.

"If you are truly interested in a scientific career come back and talk to me about it when your marks are in the 90's. I promise you I will listen."

Nineties? He might as well have said she could come back when she'd sprouted wings. She bit her lip and stared at the floor.

Master Bix looked at her frowningly, and then sighed. "The dinner bell has gone, I believe. You'd better run along. Your floor is on house duty this month, isn't it? They'll be missing you."

They missed her all right, and showed her with angry glares. "Hurry, get into your overall. Now take this." A tureen of scalding soup was thrust into her hands. "And don't dawdle. All the rolls have still to be put out."

For the next hour there was no time for thought or

boredom or anything else. Liza sped from stove to serving hatch. She barely had time to grab a bowl of soup and a protein biscuit before it was time to put out the desserts and the big urns full of herb tea.

As soon as dinner was over the kitchen staff hurried out to clear the tables and wipe them down. For the rest of the City the time after dinner was the relaxing time, the time to talk with friends or catch up on the latest scientific gossip. After the first cup of tea the talking would die down and the music would begin. There were two violinists among the older mathematicians, and an elderly flautist from Biology. None of the younger people could play anything. Since the coming of the ring there had been no time for the arts, no time for anything but work.

Liza couldn't carry a tune, but she liked to listen to the way the music seemed to wind in and out and finish off in the right place. Only tonight the pile of pots and pans was even bigger than usual, and though the others had finished washing the plates and putting them away, none of them offered to help her . . . her fault for being late, she supposed.

She stood elbow-deep in greasy water scrubbing and scraping, while only an occasional snatch of music reached her. Hateful pots! Long ago, in the days before the ring, there had been automatic dishwashers. Though how a machine could scour and rinse she couldn't imagine. Perhaps it was just a story. There were many stories about the old days, the days when the sun shone in winter and there was fuel to burn and even to waste.

At last the pots were done and hung in place. The sinks were emptied into the reclamation tanks in the basement. Liza cleaned off the greasy tide-mark, hung up the cloths and brushes to dry and washed her hands. At last. She whipped off her overall, and then remembered the shame of her red winter uniform.

Maybe Master Bix had only been concerned about her catching cold, but it was a horrible punishment, proclaiming to the whole City that Liza Monroe was different.

11

She lurked in the kitchen, just behind the serving hatch, where she could hear the music and not be seen. The violins were playing a dancing kind of music, and it was impossible to keep her feet still. Yet out there everyone sat around the neat dining tables and there wasn't a stamping foot to be seen. To be sure a few people moved their hands gently to the rhythm, and old Doctor Merriman's head wagged in time. But then he was so old his head wagged anyway.

I am *so* depressed, thought Liza, leaning her head against the frame of the serving hatch. She saw herself twenty years older, even *forty*, sitting at a table in this same dining room, with the same faces around, only older and wrinkled, as hers would be too. And nothing whatever to look forward to – except the darkness of winter beneath the shadow of the ring, and the threat of the ice creeping closer every year.

And now this winter was upon them, with nothing to look at but the walls of the City. Why couldn't girls go outside in winter? It couldn't be *that* bad. The scientists went out on field trips right up to the very edge of the ice-field. Why not she? If she were a man she would be allowed to go, even if her marks weren't too good. If only...

At that moment the Great Idea was born, while Liza leaned against the frame of the hatch and listened to the violins.

Suppose she were to stow away on an expedition – the very next expedition – and make sure she wasn't found until they were far enough away from the City to make return impracticable. Then they'd have to let her stay, and then she'd show those men just how useful she could be...

She dreamed until the scrape of chairs brought her back to reality. But now reality was bearable. With her secret plan glowing inside her she went upstairs to her sleeping unit, not even noticing the stares and giggles at her appearance.

When Win said, "Next time you borrow my comb you could at least have the courtesy to remove your *hairs*," all she replied was,

"Sorry. I was in such a hurry."

"You're always in a hurry, Liza," Janet put in. "Why can't

you be more organized? You left your filthy clothes in a pile on the floor. Leaves and dirt!"

"And *what* is that tying up your sandal? *My* hair ribbon! Really, Liza, it's too bad of you. It's ruined."

"Oh, Letty, I am sorry. Only Master Bix was waiting..."

"Where were you? What was all the fuss about anyway?"

"Outside, that's all. Only they shut the Summer Door and I couldn't get back."

"Outside? You must be crazy!" Win stared.

"Crazy!" Letty echoed.

"Why would you *want* to go outside. There's nothing out there but cold and emptiness and..." Janet stopped and shivered.

"And adventure," Liza added, her eyes shining.

2

Ten days after the first snowfall of winter Liza sat crouched in the space she had made for herself inside one of the container sleds. Her body was doubled up, a corner of a food pack was sticking into her side, and it was getting abominably stuffy. She had to keep reminding herself: I'll actually be Outside during ringset. What fun!

She felt she had a lot to be proud of. She had organized her escape perfectly. The first thing she had done was to tell John she forgave him for not unlocking the Summer Door in time and getting her into trouble with Master Bix. Then she sat with him after supper, as soon as the pots and pans were put away, and listened to him boasting that he was the youngest man in the City to be chosen for an expedition Outside.

"Tell me exactly where you're going and what you're going to do?" she had asked eagerly, and John had glowed and begun to talk and talk... None of his room-mates showed any interest in his good luck, and being the youngest

13

had some disadvantages; nobody else seemed to find him in the least bit important or understand what a big event the first time Out was in a fellow's life.

"We'll head due north, right up to the foot of the glaciers. You know that there've been teams up there all summer measuring the shrinkage of the ice? Well, now it's very important to have a record of how quickly the glacier starts growing forward again."

"I thought the ice-field was coming closer to us all the time, summer and winter."

"That's true. As more snow solidifies on the ice-field the weight on top makes the lower parts creep forward. But in the middle of summer the sun melts the forward edge faster than it creeps forward, so it seems as if the ice-field is retreating. But it isn't, of course, worse luck. This summer it hardly melted at all."

"And after ringset I suppose the north is so cold with no sunshine getting through, that the ice grows really fast? It's scary!" Liza wasn't really acting when she shivered. The thought of the whole world being buried under ice, even if it were far in the future, was a shivery thought.

John suddenly put his hand over hers. It was comforting, warm and large and capable. Liza felt a most unexpected flutter inside. How nice it would be to have someone like John to rely on...

But no! She drew her hand away. She wasn't going to turn into a typical housewoman, without an idea of her own. She was going to think her own thoughts, have her own adventures.

"They say that within ten years the ice-field will be right on top of us. That the City will be sealed under the ice for ever." We'll have to move then, she thought. Away from this boring City.

"Don't be scared." John didn't understand that her voice shook with excitement, not fear. "We'll come up with something to reverse the cold. It's not just us, after all. There are cities like ours all round the northern hemisphere – Scandinavia, Russia, China, Alaska. We're bound to find an answer."

"Suppose we don't? Where will we go?"

"South, of course. There *is* no other direction."

"And build new Cities? On and on. Won't we run out of raw materials and energy?"

"Yes, we will." John looked at Liza in surprise. "Hey, how do you know all this? The next five years are critical. If we don't slow down the advance of the ice in that time there'll *be* no slowing down. That's why this winter's expeditions are so important. By next ringrise the computer will be able to predict exactly how fast the field will move in the next five years."

"And you're going on the first expedition! I wish I could see all the equipment, everything."

"Pretty dull stuff."

Liza's brain worked rapidly. "Not to me. I'd like to be able to visualize what it'll be like, when you're out there. Seeing the equipment would make it all more real."

John went bright red. "Come on then. I'll show you now. There'll be nobody about."

He grabbed her hand. Nobody paid any attention as they walked out of the dining room, and the big hall was empty. Under the shadow of the main stairs was a door marked 'Authorized Personnel Only'.

John looked around and then opened the door. "Quick!"

Liza was impressed. "What'll you do if they catch us?"

"I'm authorized personnel. And anyway who's going to make a fuss if I show my best girl the storage floor." He put his arm round her waist. Liza shrank back. But she did want to see if her plan could possibly work, and for this she needed John. She relaxed and they went down the stairs with his arm round her waist, rather awkwardly, as their hips kept bumping.

Another door at the bottom opened with a push. Liza stepped beyond it and looked round curiously. This was not women's territory, and she had never been down here before. It was a huge space, broken only by support pillars and lit

15

dimly by permanent lighting. It looked like a dead forest of cement trees, straight lines of them retreating in every direction until the lines were lost in shadow.

"Nobody's down here." John's voice echoed weirdly in the vault. "Come on. I'll show you where we're loading up. A lot of that's *my* job, you know."

"All this?" Liza stared at the stacks of neat cartons, each of them colour-coded and marked with stencilled numbers.

"We'll be gone for a whole month, you know. We have to be entirely self-sufficient. No one can live Outside after ringset."

"What about Ekoes?"

"I've never met anyone who's actually seen one. I think they're just a myth. Maybe in the old days, before the ring, people lived in the far north, but it seems pretty unlikely. And they certainly couldn't now."

Liza was a little disappointed. The legends about the savage hairy creatures, who could talk to animals and who lived under the snow, was one of the exciting things about Outside.

"I suppose you're right," she said reluctantly.

"Of course I am." John was confident. "Here's where I'm working. Each sled is numbered, and there's a list of the equipment to go in each: scientific equipment, clothing for Outside, food for a month, and fuel for the snowmobiles and for cooking and heating ... see, these containers, red for petrol and orange for kerosene."

"Goodness, I've never seen so much fuel all at once. Where did you get it?"

"All the world shares with us. We're all in the same boat. Even OPEC sends us special rations for glacier research. After all, if we fail, the ice will cover Europe again and everyone will be pushed across the Mediterranean into North Africa and the Middle East. They don't want *that* to happen."

"At least the Europeans will have somewhere to go. But what about us, John? Where will we go? The States have got enough problems with food shortages now the weather's

16

changed, and they won't want us."

"It mustn't happen, that's all. And if we can't stop the ice up here in Canada, the States will be under ice as well, in less than a hundred years. We have to stop it, for the sake of the whole world. If we don't we'll lose everything. We'll be back where we started ten thousand years ago."

"Oh, rats!" Liza shook her red hair out of her eyes. She forgot to be sweet and polite. "Man won't go under that easily. I bet we'd remember things. And next time we'd jump ahead faster, that's all."

John frowned and looked put out, and Liza remembered the role she was playing and why. She smiled. "But it won't happen, will it? You'll stop the ice."

"You bet we will. Stop the ice or break up the ring. The Americans and Russians are working together on that part of it from the Space Station." He took her arm. "Look, these are the sleds I'm loading right now."

Liza looked closely at the boxlike sleds. They were mounted on wide runners, and were hitched in a line, one behind the other, half a dozen to be pulled by one of the huge snowmobiles which would also be home and laboratory for the scientists while they were Outside. She looked, and the Plan jumped into her head, complete in every detail. She looked closely at the fastenings of the sled door, wondered about the possibility of making air-holes. It wouldn't do to suffocate . . .

There was silence and she saw that John was staring at her. She blinked and laughed. "I'm sorry. Did you say something?"

"My goodness, you were light years away. You didn't hear a word."

"I was imagining what it would be like to be out there. I'm impressed, John, really."

He drew himself up and stuck his thumbs in the waistband of his tunic. "It *is* impressive, isn't it? Makes one proud to be part of the City."

"If I could only go too," Liza dreamed, out loud, just

17

testing him. If she could get John to help her it would certainly be much easier.

But he only laughed. "A girl Outside after ringset? That's the wildest idea I've ever heard. Women aren't strong enough to stand the terrible conditions," he explained kindly. "And you know we need you here to keep the City running smoothly."

Which was true enough, Liza thought resentfully. A full day's work in the kitchen would have him on his knees. Well, she knew where she stood. She would have to work out her plan alone.

"Only joking," she said. "I'm sure Outside must be horribly uncomfortable. Imagine not being able to wash my hair for a whole month! But you were asking me something before, weren't you?"

"I was? . . . oh, yes. I just wondered if you'd seen enough. We could go upstairs and play backgammon if you liked."

Liza was tempted. She could beat most of her friends with her eyes shut. It would be interesting to take on John. But she wasn't finished down here yet.

"I'd rather see more. For instance, what do you wear? They say that a person'll be dead from cold after five minutes Outside after ringset. It isn't really true, is it?"

"A bit exaggerated, but if it's very cold and there's a strong wind it doesn't take long to freeze flesh. But we're well protected, don't worry. I'll show you."

He led her down aisles piled with equipment. "For measuring temperature, wind-speed, sun-strength . . . "

"But there *is* no sun after ringset . . . "

"The sun's still there, silly. Even if we can't see it because of the ring. Sure, only about a quarter of its energy reaches Earth, and that's what we have to measure precisely, so the computer can tell us just how long we have."

"You mean . . . maybe not as long as five years?"

John shrugged. "The Norwegians think we're too optimistic. We hope they're wrong."

"I hope so." Liza shivered. The reality was suddenly closer, down among the equipment. The City was so warm and secure that it was hard to remember the danger that threatened them all, that was the reason for the City's existence.

"Cold?"

"A bit. There's not much heat down here, is there?"

"No need for it. Equipment stores better at lower temperatures, especially when it's designed for Outside. Look what we've got here. Try this on and see if it stops the shivers."

Liza shrugged into the jacket John held out for her. It was light, quilted with something soft and puffy between its layers. She hugged it to her chest. "It's lovely."

"There are trousers too, and mitts and socks. And over here are headmasks. They cover everything except for your eyes, and if conditions are really bad we've got goggles to protect them."

"This clothing'll really keep you warm Outside?"

"Warm enough for the length of time it takes to make readings. In between we're in the snowmobile cab, as snug as can be. I'm really looking forward to it!"

Me too, Liza thought silently. Wouldn't John be surprised when she popped up out of one of the sleds! She'd have to stay hidden long enough, maybe into the second day, so that they couldn't turn round and take her back. She hid a smile and took off the quilted jacket. There was only one more thing to find out...

"So when do you leave?" She smiled up at John. "Maybe I'll come and wave goodbye."

"Promise?"

"Oh, I won't do that. Something might come up. But I promise I'll be thinking of you, the whole way." And *that*'s true anyway, she thought, and tried not to giggle.

John blushed. She saw his adam's apple bob up and down as he swallowed. "You know, Liza, I've never had a girl friend before – I mean, someone special. It'll make all the difference Outside, knowing someone's thinking about me."

Liza felt suddenly uncomfortable, she wasn't sure why.

After all, it was just a game, wasn't it? She pushed the feeling to the back of her mind. Later, perhaps, she'd think about it. Right now . . . she looked up at John. He was tall and really not too bad-looking. She made herself smile. "Well, when *do* you start?"

"In four days."

"Early, I suppose?"

"We'll be up and fed and on our way by six. You'll have to wake up earlier than that if you're going to wave goodbye to me."

She smiled but didn't answer. Her mind was working busily. I'll have to hide the night before, she thought, as they walked along the dim aisles. But how am I going to stop the girls from reporting me missing as soon as they see my empty bed? If there's an alarm John will remember all these questions and then . . . I've got to think of a good reason for not being in my own bed. And I'd better get hold of extra food and drink, in case I have to hide in a sled with no food stores. And what about sanitary arrangements? Maybe a bucket or something? I'll never last a whole day and night without . . .

They climbed the stairs in silence, each of them busy with their very different thoughts. When Liza put out her hand to push open the door at the top John stopped her and pulled her abruptly against him and kissed her hard, right on the lips.

It felt bristly and she couldn't breathe. She struggled and he let her go at once. Then she felt sad, as if she were turning her back on something that might be very important. She ran through the door and straight up the main staircase to her own room. Her mind was whirling and her heart pounded. John? And her? She hadn't seriously thought of the two of them that way before. And she wasn't going to now. Now she must concentrate her whole mind on planning how to join the expedition. Forget about John. Later, perhaps, when it was all over. But as she fell asleep she found herself running her fingers over her lips. They felt different.

But she forgot her new feelings as she puzzled over how

she was going to get away without being noticed. Janet and Win and Lettie were always there. Always watching. Always ready to criticize. There wasn't a place in the City that was really private, she thought irritably. She was sick and tired of it!

Then a blindingly beautiful idea hit her. She'd pretend to be sick that night and go to the hospital, away from the girls' prying eyes. She'd eat secretly and then at mealtimes she'd push the food around her plate and say she didn't feel too good.

She did this for two days, and then on the evening before the expedition was due to leave she complained of having a pain.

They were just undressing for bed. "You'd better go and see the doctor," Win said kindly. "Would you like me to go with you?"

"Don't fuss," said Liza rudely. The last thing she needed was a helping hand. "I'm tired, and those yeast cakes were too fatty, that's all."

"You didn't even touch yours, I noticed. You just cut them up and pushed them around your plate. Waste of good food, really."

"Good lord, you sound just like a house Mother! Don't fuss. If I feel ill in the morning I'll report to the hospital."

Win shrugged and turned her back, offended. Liza climbed into bed and lay still, pretending to be asleep. She must wait until it was quite late, until she was sure that the corridors would all be empty.

The hours dragged by. Once she fell asleep and woke with a jerk, afraid that the morning had come and she had missed her chance. But the City was silent. She lay and listened to the quiet breathing of the other three.

She eased herself cautiously out of bed. Janet stirred. "Wah?"

"Sh! Go back to sleep. My stomach hurts, that's all. I'm going to the hospital."

Janet struggled up on one elbow, her eyes still shut. "You

all right? D'you need help?" Her voice slurred.

"I'm fine. Go back to sleep," Liza whispered.

Janet's head dropped back to her pillow. Good! Now she had a sure alibi. And she'd annoyed the girls enough so they wouldn't bother to check on how she was for a while.

She slid out of the room, still in her pyjamas. It was a crazy way to start out on an expedition . . . pyjamas and not even a toothbrush! She padded barefoot along the silent corridor, lit only by dim night-lights. How strange it felt to be up while the whole City lay dreaming, secure and shuttered, under the Hill. Liza felt like a trespasser as she tiptoed down the stairs and slid into the deeper darkness of the shadow beneath them.

There was the door. It opened without a creak and she slipped through and closed it behind her. At the foot of the dimly lit stairs, the space seemed to stretch away in every direction in a forest of pillars and shadows.

Liza forced herself to stop and listen, just to be sure. There was no sound except for her own heart, thumping away like mad. Did she remember the direction? You could wander around for hours between these rows of identical pillars.

But it was all right. Her feet took her without mistake directly to the shelves of polar clothing, and she pulled on padded trousers and jacket and socks, all a little too big. It took a long time to find a pair of boots that fitted well enough for her to be able to walk properly. Then the helmet, that would cover everything but her eyes, and a pair of goggles.

With these in her hand she went to look for the best place to hide. The sleds were lined up, already linked to their snowmobiles, facing the passage that led up through the Hill to the Winter Door high on the southeastern hillside. The first sleds she inspected were so crammed with equipment that you couldn't have hidden a mouse in them, much less a full grown girl. How awful if they were all like that. She daren't take out a piece of equipment that might be essential to the expedition.

She walked slowly down the train, opening and closing the

sled doors. Right at the very back was one that held only containers of food and cans of kerosene. Obviously there wasn't enough for a full load, and some quilts had been pushed in between the cans to stop them from shifting.

Perfect! Liza pulled out one of the quilts and a couple of kerosene cans, and there was a nest-shaped place, just big enough for her to curl up in. And it was really quite comfortable, she told herself, after she'd tried it out; and she could cover herself with one of the quilts in case anyone checked the load.

She hid the spare quilt and the cans of kerosene among the stacks of equipment on one of the other aisles, and then went up to the kitchen to get enough food and water to last her through the first day. She didn't take much, just a flask of water and half a dozen soy patties wrapped in a towel. And a small pail with a lid, which would be horrible to use, but not for long, after all.

Back downstairs again she checked the fastening of the sled door. It was large and clumsy, obviously made to be used by men wearing heavy mitts. If she could find a tool, a screwdriver perhaps, she'd be able to open it from the inside. Just in case they didn't hear her yelling at the end of the second day.

She found one without any trouble, and while she was at it she used the sharp end to make a couple of air-holes in the plastic top of the sled. All she would have to do was climb in and somehow fasten the tongue of the latch over the hasp on the side of the door. She worked out a way of doing it with a loop of string around the tongue. She tried it out a couple of times, snapping the tongue onto the hasp and then jerking the string free. It worked beautifully.

Now there was nothing to do but wait. How long? She didn't own a watch. They weren't needed in a City governed by bells, and one got an instinct for the right time. But down here it was all different. In the darkness and the silence time seemed to be stretching out into a rubbery softness that went on and on . . .

She had one of the quilts between her and the door, and

others around her back and sides. It was quite comfortable, but abominably stuffy in spite of the air-holes. She found that she couldn't bear to wait with the door completely shut, not just yet. So she sat with the door ajar and the string in her hand. She would yank it shut the instant the main lights came on and she heard voices. There'd be plenty of time.

The winter suit and the bundle of quilts were soft and warm, and the night was long. Soon her eyes shut and her head nodded until her cheek came to rest against her knees. She slept.

She woke to a bewildering roar of engines and the hollow echo of many voices. Before she had time to move the partly open door was discovered. She heard an exclamation of annoyance, and shrank back into stillness.

The door was pulled all the way open. She felt the sudden gush of cold air, though she could see nothing behind her quilt. The padding was tucked in more firmly. A hand actually touched her foot. Then the door slammed. She heard the snap of the fastening, and when she peeked through the quilt she was in total darkness.

For just an instant she panicked. There was the horrible sensation of being trapped, not only within the sled, but within a series of events over which she suddenly had no more control. She swallowed and made herself breathe slowly until the fear subsided. After all, this was what she wanted, wasn't it? *This* was excitement!

The sled trembled and moved. She could feel as well as hear the protesting whine of runner against polished floor. Then she was on a slope, moving more easily. They used foam in the passage, she remembered, to simulate the snow for which the runners of the sleds were designed. She tilted over to her left as they laboured upward. This sensation, and the enormous thudding roar of the labouring snowmobile engine in the enclosed space, seemed to go on for ever. An ugly smell drifted through her air-holes and her eyes began to smart.

Then, at last, she was level again and it was quiet. She

24

listened hard, and heard faintly the sound of voices and the distant clang of a big door closing. The Winter Door. The sled vibrated, and they were off again, moving smoothly over the fresh snow. On their way north!

Liza had no idea how far or how fast they travelled, and she could get no clue from her hiding place. Through her breathing holes she could see no more than two tiny circles of grey sky that never seemed to change. If it were not for the faint continuous vibration she would have supposed that the sled was standing still. Like needles of ice the wind pierced the air-holes, and she pushed a fold of the quilt against the roof, and only uncovered the holes for a few minutes at a time when she could bear the stuffiness of the sled no longer.

She ate two of the soy patties and had a very small drink of water, more for something to pass the time than because she was hungry. Then she slept again, jolting a little as the sled moved over older snow, wind-sculptured and winter-hardened into waves.

She woke with her bottom numb and her thighs and knees aching from the cramped position she had held for so many hours. When she looked out of her air-holes there seemed to be no difference between the darkness within and the dark outside. Was it really night? Yet still they travelled north. Did they ever intend to stop? Suppose they went all the way up to the ice-field without stopping? What on earth would she do? It had never occurred to her that they might be taking it in turn to drive the big snowmobiles, the others sleeping in the bunks of the cabs.

Oh, how good a bunk would feel. A place to stretch out in. A chance to ease the pain in her legs, her back, her neck. Was the night ever going to end? She ate a little more, but she felt unsatisfied. What she'd really like would be a big bowl of hot stew, full to the brim of summer vegetables and synthetic protein. Her mouth watered at the thought.

At last it was daylight again. Once more she could see grey through the small holes in the roof. If they didn't stop by evening she was going to yell. But would they hear her? If they didn't she could prise open the door and jump down and get their attention that way. Only she wasn't sure how fast they were moving. Suppose it was faster then she could run? She might be left behind. That was a scary thought to occupy the mind.

She cried a little, she was feeling so low and her legs ached so badly. Then she dozed. She woke to feel that something had changed, but for a minute she wasn't sure what.

The sled had stopped! That was it. The second evening must have come already. She had slept the whole afternoon away. She tensed herself. Now was the moment. Now she must climb out and show herself. They'd be dreadfully angry. She hadn't really *thought* before just how angry they were going to be. Oh, dear. But they couldn't go back to the City, not after two days and a night. Not possibly. They'd have to take her along. And that was going to be worth all the scoldings in the world. And wouldn't John be surprised to see her!

She groped on the floor for the screwdriver. Bother. It must have rolled to the back while they were going up the tunnel to the Winter Door. Her hands fumbled among the folds of quilt. There it was.

There was a sudden clatter and voices close by. Should she call out or prise open the door and really surprise them? She slid the screwdriver into the crack between the door and the sled wall. The plastic flange pushed aside easily against the tool. But why was it so stiff? It had been simple enough to open before. Was it the cold? Had the latch frozen?

"Sure we'll find it again?" One of the men must be standing right in front of the door. She heard him cough and spit. There was another voice, further away.

" ... homing signal ... flag ... under two metres of snow by the time ... " The voices moved off.

Liza pushed harder, forcing the screwdriver up against the latch. She heard an engine rev up. "Hey, I'm here!" She yelled.

The engine's noise changed as it geared down. So they

26

weren't staying here. Maybe it wasn't evening after all. They were going on and she'd missed her chance to get out of this cramped sled. She could have cried with frustration and the pain in her legs.

She braced herself for the starting jerk. It never came. She could hear the screech of runners across cold snow and the steady throb of snowmobile engines. The sounds grew fainter. There was nothing but silence. Nothing except the sound of her breathing and the movement of her body against the quilts.

"Come back! You can't leave me here. Hey, come back!"

Desperately she pushed the screwdriver against the door latch and hit it hard with her other fist. It didn't budge. This was like the worst kind of nightmare come true. *Was* it true? She tried to swallow the fear that rose bitter in her throat. She stopped to wipe the sweat out of her eyes and off her hands, and pushed and levered at the latch again. But still the door would not budge. She was not only alone Outside. She was trapped!

3

The silence was as profound as it must be in the sky beyond the ring, Liza thought. At first there were small sounds: her boot rasping against the floor of the sled, and a dry crepitating noise close to her ear that terrified her into stillness. When she dared to move she realised it was the sound of her own eyelashes brushing against the stretched surface of the quilt where it touched her face.

After a while these tiny sounds no longer registered, and the silence became a smothering blanket that covered her. The blackness inside the sled was no longer just an absence of light, but an actual substance, sticky and dark, that filled every crack and cranny and threatened to crawl into eyes and ears and mouth.

Liza was fifteen years old, and she had never really been alone in her whole life. In the City babies shared the same nursery, the same dormitory, attended the same play school. When they were old enough to leave the children's dormitory, it was in exchange for a room to be shared with three others. Even the showers were communal.

To be truly alone in the City one had to lock oneself in a lavatory, and even that did not shut out the City sounds. Bells, clattering feet, voices. Busyness surrounded them from wake-up to lights-out. At night. Yes, one was most alone at night. In the near darkness. Listening to the sleeping sounds of Win and Janet and Letty . . .

What are they doing now? she thought. Will they miss me now I'm gone? Will anyone? Probably not. Even her own parents would not be affected by her absence. Her relationship with Master Bix was more personal than that with her father; and her feelings for Marianne Battray, the chief woman on her floor, were stronger than her feelings for her mother. No, nobody would care. Nobody would mourn. A tear of self-pity ran stickily down Liza's cheek. She sniffed and scrubbed it angrily away.

I won't die, she said out loud. I can't die. It's too stupid, too much of a waste. I haven't done a single useful thing, and I'm not going to be remembered as a horrid example of what happens to girls who get ideas above themselves. I won't just sit here and die!

She struggled out of the enveloping folds of quilt and managed to push them out of the way behind her. She needed room and breathing space. She wiped her right hand down the length of her quilted jacket and grasped the screwdriver firmly. It had worked back in the City. It should work now. She tried to visualize the way the tongue fitted in the groove and the way the hasp snapped down over it to prevent it from flying open at every jolt on the journey. Was there something more that she had missed? Perhaps another fastening?

Liza didn't pray. There were no gods in the City, unless

you chose to call Science a god. But as she levered the screwdriver against the lock her mind said: Please let it open. Don't let me be trapped inside here until I die. Please . . .

She pushed against the latch, wriggling around until all her weight was against the door and her feet were braced against the piled cartons. She pushed and prised desperately. Something gave. There was a sudden CRACK. The door swung open and she rolled head over heels into the burning cold of the snow.

She gasped at the cold and tried to scramble to her feet, but her legs collapsed under her, and she had to cling to the edge of the opening until the feeling in them came back. In spite of the pain she laughed. She was free and she wasn't going to die! Not yet anyway, a thought intruded. She pushed it out of the way and looked around her curiously.

So this was the northland! It stretched white and featureless in every direction. The sky was grey and overcast, hiding the ring. The most real thing was the cold wind pouring, as solid as a sheet of water, out of the north. Even as she stood staring about her the sound of it rose to a scream, whipping the loose snow from the surface of the land as it passed, so that it seemed that the whole country was smoking, an icy white smoke.

Liza looked back, the way the expedition had come. The parallel troughs of sled runners and the patterns of snow-mobile treads made a shadow road, grey on paler grey, that led as straight as a ruler back towards the City. When she looked north she could see the same pattern vanishing into the smoky distance.

What was she to do? Try and return to the City, or follow in the tracks of the expedition and hope it would not be too long before they stopped again? Even while she stood there, hesitating, the blown snow smoked knee high, rising and falling in whirling columns of white. As she watched the trail faded, vanished. There was no going forward, no going back.

The cold reached up through Liza's body from her legs,

calf-deep in snow, to her middle, and turned her stomach to ice. It numbed her chest and her shoulders, her head. Now her brain didn't work properly any more. There was nothing in the world but the howl of the wind and the harsh whisper of snow driven hard against the walls of the sled. She needed to sleep. To lie down, to curl up under the soft blanket of white snow, to shut out the buffeting torment of the wind. To sleep...

As her knees buckled, her hand dragged over the broken metal fastening of the sled door. The jagged edge caught her wrist and the sudden pain jerked her back to reality. She musn't sleep here. The snow was death. She must get out of the snow!

With legs stiff and numb with cold she clambered clumsily up inside the sled and wrapped the quilts around her. The wind tugged incessantly at the open door. She managed to loop the piece of string she had brought through the broken latch, pull the door to, and hold it closed.

Now the stuffiness inside the sled was bliss. Liza huddled within the quilts. Slowly the warmth crept back into her body. She slept.

She woke hungry and thirsty. When she slackened the loop of string that held the door she could see through the crack that it was daylight, that the sky was clear and the wind had died. The still cold air sliced like a knife through the comfortable fug of the sled. She pulled the door shut again and felt around for a meal package.

She ate the whole ration, yeast rolls, a block of tofu, a fresh tomato from the hydroponic garden, and a bottle of hi-pro drink. When the container was empty she felt a bit more cheerful and able to face thinking about the future.

What was she going to do? She was a dot, a zero, in an illimitable expanse of snow. She knew vaguely that the expedition had been heading north. Equally vaguely she knew that the City lay somewhere to the south. And that was the sum total. If she left the sled she would have nothing to hang on to. It was her only reality.

She began to feel a bit sick. Maybe she shouldn't have eaten so much all at once. Other questions crowded her mind. Why had her particular sled been dropped off halfway through the second day? As a supply depot for the return trip, her mind answered quickly. If they were to drop off a container every day or so on the way up to the ice-field, the load would become progressively lighter and they would make better time at less fuel cost. But why hadn't John told her that? And why, oh why had she been so unlucky as to pick the sled that would be dropped off first? Because you picked the last sled in the line, stupid, her mind answered uncompromisingly. Nothing to do with luck.

Could she survive until they returned to pick up this last sled? That was the vital question. Enough food for twenty scientists for two days would be enough for her for a month and a half. Didn't John say that they planned to be Outside for a month? Water would be a problem. Perhaps she could use empty food containers, fill them with snow and keep them in the sled to melt with her body temperature. She wouldn't get much that way. Perhaps there was firewood out there in the whiteness. There was plenty of kerosene to start a fire, though what a waste...

Liza stopped her planning as a new and awful thought came to her mind. If she ate the supplies and used up precious fuel to melt snow, then what would the expedition do when they got back to this cache? If she used it all up they would be two days without food. That was bad enough. But if they were counting on the kerosene for stoves and she used it up ... it could be the death of every one of them.

I won't use the fuel, she swore. Not a drop. I'll manage without. And I'll eat as little as I can. Oh, I'm sorry. I didn't mean to. She sniffed and rubbed her eyes. I did it again, she thought savagely. I just didn't think ahead. Dumb, dumb!

After a long time she slept, and when she woke it was morning again, the short grudging morning of the northland winter. She ate a very little, just enough to take away the empty pain, and then climbed out into the snow.

Nothing had changed in this unchanging land. It stretched away, shadowless in every direction, shadowless because of the presence of that greater shadow, the shadow of the ring, that lay sombrely over the whole northern hemisphere. The flat light made it difficult to see contours. Were those low hills over to the west? Perhaps something lay beyond them. It was worth going to look anyway. It was something to do.

The sled was bright orange, the only spot of colour except for the small copper disc of the sun obscured behind the dust particles of the ring. I'll walk west for as long as I can still see the sled, she thought. And then make a circle southward and towards the east. Then maybe north. But she dreaded the idea of the north. North was where the cold came from.

She put on helmet and mitts and set out. Walking was a labour. At times the icy crust held her. Then, unexpectedly, she would plunge up to her knees in softer snow. The men would have brought skis, of course. She had heard of them, but she wouldn't have known how to use them even if she'd thought of it.

She laboured westward. There was a rise in the ground. From the crest of it she could see the sled, square and orange and very small. Extraordinarily small for something so very important. She kept looking over her shoulder, to keep an eye on it. If she lost sight of it for an instant and got turned around in this white nothingness, she would lose it for ever.

The view to the west was disappointing, a vista of low hills, a greyness without end. It made her feel very small and very alone. She turned and trudged southward, keeping the sled in sight to her left all the time. South was where the City lay. Surely there would be some sign of the civilization that had once been here? She dared a little farther, trusting to her footprints to get her safely back to the sight of the sled.

But there was nothing. A flatness broken only by the charcoal smudge of the ring. What had she hoped for? A miracle? As she turned her back on the dark bow that arched across the sullen sky she felt a great lump of loneliness in her middle. The sky was as cold and clear as green ice. A small wind moaned along the snow, rustling the powdery surface, blurring the clear line of her tracks.

She tried to hurry, stumbling, falling forward. Suppose the wind were to rise suddenly as it had done before? Suppose it were to blot out the sight of the sled? Surely she ought to be able to see it by now? Surely she hadn't gone *that* far?

Her heart bumped against her ribs, and the cold air knifed agonizingly into her lungs as she struggled along. Oh, there it was! There. Comforting, squat, brightly orange. *Home*.

Something bulky moved from behind the sled. Something dark and furry. A bear? Could it be a bear? She'd seen pictures of them. Like this. Dark, furry. And *big*. With teeth and claws, enormous claws. She had no weapon. Nothing. And there was no place to run, except to the sled. Towards the furry thing, whatever it was.

The creature had seen her now. It was facing her, waving its front paws menacingly. Did it smell her? Was she *food*? Or was it merely curious? Liza's mind began to work again. She had only one chance, and that was to dodge around the sled on the opposite side to the creature, and then duck quickly inside. If she could move more quickly than it. If she could hold the door tightly shut against those claws. If . . .

She plunged down the slight slope towards the sled, her head down, her eyes on the surface of the snow. So long as she didn't fall into a drift . . . There. She was almost at the sled. She ran around the other side. The snow had drifted here, deeper than she had expected. She wallowed, suddenly slowed down, and almost met the beast head on as *it* doubled back to meet her.

She gasped and turned back. Around the sled. Now she was at the door. Now her knee was on the floor of the sled, her hands pulling at the sides of the door. She kicked herself forward into the blessed safety of the inside.

Only something was pulling her back. Even through her heavy quilted jacket she could feel two furry paws at her waist, lifting her down, turning her round so that she was face to face with it.

What was she expecting? Sharp canines, a red slavering mouth, angry little eyes...?

Liza had never fainted in her life before, and when she began to come to her senses she wasn't sure what had happened. She was lying flat on her back, and close to her ear was an unfamiliar sound, a continuous swish-swish, half hiss, half whine. She tried to move, but she couldn't. Was she tied? She could lift her head a couple of centimetres, no more, and that was it.

She peered down the length of her body and saw that she was wrapped in fur, animal fur. There was a pungent smell in her nostrils, and her face felt fur against it when she tried to move. She was lying on something, covered with fur and bound down with leather straps.

As she stared her mind made the jump. She was on a kind of rough sled with no top, that was it. Ahead of her, into the wind, half hidden in a cloud of their own hot breath, was a string of lean hairy animals – could they be wolves? It was they that were pulling the sled, fast, unbelievably fast, so that its runners screamed across the protesting crystals of snow.

Liza shut her eyes tight. It must be a bad dream. Soon she would wake up and find herself in her bed in the City. Or even back in the storage sled. That wouldn't be too bad. Anything would be better than *this*. And what of the bear? Had it been real, or was it part of the same dream?

Her eyes flew open. The bear! But it hadn't been a bear after all, had it? There was a muddled memory, in the instant before fainting, of a wide smile with white human-sized teeth, dark eyes and brown cheeks, smooth and shining with grease. But he seemed to have vanished, if he had ever really been there. She could see nothing but this rough wooden sled and the wild wolves racing with her across the northland.

An Eko had caught her. That was what had happened. It was all true. He had appeared first as a bear and then had turned himself into a pack of wolves. Ekoes... All the nursery tales came tumbling back into her mind.

Ekoes lived in the uninhabitable land of ice. They could turn themselves at will into animals and then back into human form. They lived beneath the snow and they ate *meat* and drank *blood* ... Be good or an Eko will get you! Don't go out after ringset or... Liza had heard lots of that when she was growing up, every time she got into trouble. Be good or... She shuddered. Meat-eaters! They probably planned to eat *her*.

The sled hurtled on, the snow rising like smoke under the runners, the breath of the wolves a cloud overhead. The grey day turned slowly into a grey twilight. Still they travelled on.

It was almost dark before the sled suddenly stopped. Out of the snow appeared a whole pack of bear-creatures, thick-furred, all standing on their hind legs and yipping shrilly. Liza struggled desperately against the bonds that held her to the sled. Better by far to run away and be lost in the snow than stay to be eaten alive.

But it was hopeless. As soon as she moved at all the furry heads turned towards her. There was a high-pitched scream and one of the bear-creatures bounded towards her, leaned over her...

Liza gulped and shut her eyes tightly.

"Ayah! Iriook?" Astonishingly it was a woman's voice, soft and so full of love and wonder that Liza's eyes shot open. The creature seemed to push back the top of its furry head with a paw, and Liza found herself staring into a woman's face, broad, brown, shining with grease and tears. *Tears?*

For a moment the whole world seemed to whirl round her. Then she realised that these were not bears at all, but *people*, clad in animal fur from head to toe, with deep hoods that hid their faces. They must be Ekoes, Liza thought, and her heart thumped. Had they ever been bears? Or had she been fooled by her own fears? The wolf pack was unchanged, if indeed they were wolves. They were now unharnessed and circled one of the strangers, yapping shrilly for the hunks of raw meat he threw to them.

A man's voice – or was it a boy's – came from behind her head. Was he speaking English? If so the accent was very strange, unlike any she'd heard in the City. What was that word he repeated? 'Spirit nest'? What could it mean?

Whatever it was it had a magic effect on the woman, whose arms reached down to hug Liza. She pushed her face forward until their noses touched, and sniffed, as if she actually wanted to smell Liza. Liza held her breath. She didn't have to sniff to be aware of the overwhelming scent of fish and rancid oil.

"Iriook!" There was that strange word again. "You have come back to me, Iriook!"

It was suddenly clear to Liza from the way the woman looked at her and held her, as much as from her words, that she thought Liza was another girl, somebody she had loved and lost, somebody called Iriook.

The woman's hands patted her all over, as if to make sure that she was all in one piece, and then began to undo the straps that bound her. "You have come back, Iriook," she repeated.

"No, no." Liza shook her head and pointed at herself with her now free hands. "I am Liza Monroe and I am from the City." She spoke slowly and pointed south, towards the centre of the ring.

There was a stir. Everyone's breath hissed between their teeth. They all stared at the ring and then at Liza.

"Ayee!" The woman clung to Liza as if afraid to let her go. "Paija took. Paija return."

They all nodded solemnly and eager hands reached out to pull off the furs. There were cries of amazement when they saw how she was dressed, and so much fast talk that she couldn't understand a word of it. Then she was lifted to her feet. Pins and needles shot agonizingly through her legs and her knees buckled.

The young man who had talked about spirit nests caught her, and she was half dragged, half carried away from the sled and suddenly pushed into what she thought was a deep snowbank. She tried to fight, remembering yet another Eko legend: THEY live under the snow and jump out on unsuspecting travellers... THEY drink their blood...

There were too many hands holding her, and the space was too cramped for her to put up anything of a fight. For a horrible instant she thought that they were going to suffocate her in the snow. Then she realised that she was being pushed along a tunnel, carved out of solid snow. She stopped struggling, and let them lift her to her feet and help her across a round room to where a shelf was piled deep and warm with pungent furs.

Above her head was a smooth white dome that reached down and turned into walls. At first she thought it was a kind of translucent stone, but when she touched it with a bare finger she realised that the whole room was made out of blocks of frozen snow. She realised too that she was seeing it because of the light coming from a small stone dish in the middle of the room, which cast moving shadows that danced on the curve above her head.

There was much bustle and talk and pushing bodies, and when it died down she found that around her on the wide shelf were about ten people, all staring at her. They pulled off their fur jackets and trousers, to reveal similar garments beneath, apparently made of leather with the fur inside against their skins. They tried to pull off her clothes too, but they did not understand how the zippers worked. Once Liza understood that they weren't going to hurt her, she took off her own parka and trousers.

The were snatched from her hands and passed around with loud exclamations. She hoped that she would get them safely back, as she certainly couldn't go outside in her pyjamas. But at the moment it seemed safer to go along with whatever they wanted, and their smiling faces seemed to mean no harm.

The woman who had called her Iriook knelt down beside her and began to rub her legs in a skilful way which got rid of the pins and needles almost at once. "Thank you. That's much better," Liza said shyly.

Everyone stared. The women broke into such a torrent of words mixed with tears that Liza couldn't understand any of it. She stared with her mouth open.

The young man spoke to her, and when he had repeated himself a few times, Liza understood that the woman was supposed to be her mother.

"She's not my mother! I've never seen her before."

"Ayah!" There were shrill cries and a stir from the people sitting so closely around her.

"She has come home without her mind!" the *mother* wept.

"Never mind, Kidlak. She will remember soon."

They are all mad, thought Liza. Her heart pounded, and in spite of the warmth of the bodies around her, she shivered.

At that moment another woman, about the same age as Kidlak, crawled backwards into the room from the tunnel entrance, so that Liza first saw furred feet and leggings, and then a round furry bottom. When she stood up Liza could see her face was so like Kidlak's that they must be sisters. She dragged a big steaming pot out of the tunnel, and set it down on the shelf among the crowd of people.

The smell was mouthwatering. Liza felt her nose twitch and her stomach tighten with hunger. She waited politely for them to serve her with a dishful of whatever the pot held. And waited. Arms outstretched. Hands dipped, shook off the excess gravy and pushed the chunks of food into mouths. Liza swallowed saliva. *Fingers!*

Kidlak, sitting next to Liza, reached into the pot and fished out a big chunk of food. She held it out, an oddly anxious look in her eyes. "Eat," she pleaded.

Liza took it from her with a shy smile. It was scaldingly hot and she nearly dropped it. Gravy ran down her wrist and she quickly licked it off. Delicious. She bit into the food. It was coarse and a bit stringy, different from anything she had ever eaten before, but it had a hot saltiness that seemed to heat her stomach and run straight into her blood. Everyone watched her. Had she broken some law of good manners? She cleaned off her chin with a finger and licked it.

"Thank you. It's very good," she said to the anxious woman.

"You should say 'Thank you, Mother'," the young man reproved.

"She's not my mother. Mother's back in the City. I told you."

"You have forgotten. Your mind will come back in time. Do you remember me?"

"I suppose you're my brother," Liza flashed sarcastically, but it passed over his head.

"No, no. I am your cousin, Namoonie. Next year I will be your husband."

Husband, thought Liza. Over my dead body!

"These are your brothers," he spoke slowly, pointing "Ottochie and Kumwartok and Ashoona."

Three faces stared solemnly up at her. They were like three different sizes of the same person, straight dark hair, black almond eyes, wide cheeks, brown shining faces.

"And your sisters, Ruthee and Soo, as you must know."

The same face again, this time with a braid of black hair hanging down in front of each ear.

Liza was so embarrassed she didn't know where to look. Five sibs! FIVE. In the City a couple was allowed one child, and if it were healthy and had a high I.Q., then a second might be permitted. But five, never!

"And these are my brothers, Tudlik and Iyola, and my sister, Quatsia. And this is *my* mother," Namoonie went on proudly, "who is Nawpachee, as you well know."

Liza found herself smiling at the woman who had brought in the pot.

"Here. Eat more. You are so thin." She was offered another delicious lump of food.

"Thank you," she said shyly. "Thank you, Nawpachee."

39

There was a sigh of satisfaction, as if her use of one of their names had released them from some kind of spell. Everyone ate and paid her no more attention. If she was still hungry she had to put her own hand in the pot. At first Liza thought this was disgusting, but nobody else minded, so why should she? It certainly saved on the washing up, she remembered, thinking of the mounds of dishes, platters, knives, forks and spoons that she had washed in her lifetime, only to have them dirtied again a few hours later. "Such a waste of time," she said sleepily.

She was full, and dropping with tiredness. The others seemed to have enormous appetites. The talking and eating went on and on. She dozed fitfully, propped up by the shoulders of her neighbours. At last the food was finished, and a wooden bowl was dipped into the pot for the last of the gravy. Each person drank their fill, dipped again and passed it to the neighbour on their left.

How unhygienic, thought Liza dreamily, imagining the face of the kitchen Mother if she should see this. But when the bowl reached her she drank from it unhesitatingly. It was good hot salty soup. She drained it, refilled it and passed it to Namoonie, who was sitting on her other side.

Once the pot was finished it was put down on the floor, and everybody sorted themselves out and found a place to sleep on the shelf among the furs. No toothbrushes, Liza thought, remembering that she had had to leave the City without hers. No washing?

For a while she listened to the unfamiliar sounds of eleven strangers sleeping, smelling the rank smell of fur mingled with the spicy gravy that still clung to her hands. Then she too slept.

She dreamed that she was back in the dormitory, square and sparse and clean with its four beds, four storage units, four chairs. She heard the waking bell and jumped up ready to tell the girls about her absurd dream; that she had smuggled herself Outside and been captured by Ekoes. But instead of answering her politely the girls started to shout a kind of gibberish, all at once.

She sat up, bewildered, and looked around, at the domed room, the cheerful crowd, all pushing and shoving and talking at once. It was only a dream! And *this* was the reality. Her clothes were given to her and she put them on, tears of disappointment running down her cheeks.

But there was little time to feel sorry for herself. They were ready and waiting for her. She struggled into her trousers, zipped up her jacket and put on her quilted helmet. Then she was pushed through the tunnel on hands and knees, and stood up outside, blinking in the sudden light.

Yesterday had seemed intensely gloomy in the shadow of the ring, but now that Liza had spent a night in the darkness of the snow house, she found the day almost bright. There were faint shadows, when you knew where to look, and the land did not seem quite so featureless.

She longed to wash, but there seemed to be no spare hot water, just a small pot boiling on a tiny fire of meagre willow twigs. Into it Nawpachee threw a handful of dry leaves, and stirred them up. Then a bowl – surely it was the same bowl from which they had drunk the soup last night – was dipped and circulated. Whatever the brew, it was comfortingly hot, with a herby tang. It washed down the piece of dry leathery food that had been handed to Liza.

Namoonie told her that it was 'caribou', which left her none the wiser. She chewed and chewed, and got a little nourishment from it, while the others bustled about. The two sleds were piled high with furs. Bowls and pots were tied on securely. It became clear to Liza that they were packing up, that this place was not home, in the way that the City was home. When she asked Namoonie where 'home' was, he waved his arm comprehensively around the wide bleak land. Perhaps he had not understood her question.

She was put on one of the sleds, wedged in with furs, all the belongings of the people piled around her. Then they set out, the sleds pulled, as before, by the animals she had thought were wolves. A cross between a wolf and a dog, she now decided; but they were just as frightening, with their howls and their great slavering mouths. All the rest, even

41

small Soo, plodded along through the snow on big flat plates made out of wood and webbing. They were clumsy looking, but the people loped along easily, keeping up with the sleds and never sinking into the snow.

After a while Liza got very bored just sitting, but when she suggested to Namoonie that she should walk too he shook his head and pointed to the coin-sized copper circle of the sun, low down in the western arm of the ring's arch. Obviously it was necessary for them to reach a certain place before dark, and they didn't want her to hold them back. But how they knew where they were, or how far they had yet to travel, Liza could not guess.

Their endurance was incredible. They travelled for the whole day without stopping, though the two small ones occasionally rode upon the second sled. They had had no food except for the strips of dry stuff and the herb tea with which they had broken their fast. The dogs, too, strained forward, as if they could smell their destination, and pulled the sleds without complaint.

Liza looked eagerly ahead. There was no sign of a city, or indeed of any dwelling. There was only a frozen creek creased into the barren land, with a small patch of scrub willow growing from its folds, as it did in the creek back home.

Down among the trees two figures moved. They really did look a bit like bears from this distance, Liza thought, blushing at her foolishness. They came closer, and the sleds stopped, the dogs snarling and biting at each other's legs. Namoonie yelled, moved among them, kicking, untangling the lines that fastened them to the sleds. Liza climbed out of her furs, and waited for the two men who approached from the creek. Her heart bumped against her ribs as they came close.

One of the men peered into her face and then turned to the woman Namoonie called Kidlak. "I thought at first..."

"Agaguk, indeed it is she. Namoonie found her close by the spirit nest."

"Nonsense, woman, she looks nothing like Iriook. Her pale skin, her eyes..." He stared at Liza, his eyes unfriendly.

"For shame, Agaguk. If an *Ino* took her to the spirit land you would not expect her to return unchanged, would you? Or even to remember who she is? But do you think I would not know my own child? And after all, who else could she be, tell me that, my man?"

Liza strained to understand the tumbling words. The poor woman's crazy, she thought uneasily. But if I'm not Iriook, I don't think that man is going to let me stay. And without their help I'm dead, now that they've taken me away from the storage sled. Perhaps I had better pretend to be Iriook, whoever she is, until I can think of a way of getting back home...

So when Kidlak turned to her and said, "You are Iriook, my child, are you not? Try and remember," she said softly, "I will try, Mother."

"There, you see, Agaguk? Child, you remember your father and your uncle, Kiawat, don't you?"

"Perhaps," Liza said, and looked at the other man. "You are Namoonie's father, aren't you?" she guessed.

"There, you see, she *does* remember. By the time she has been back in our world until the sun escapes from the Mouth of Paija she will have remembered everything."

The man who was Iriook's father shrugged and turned away. "We shall see," he said. His unfriendliness was very different from the warmth of the others, who now crowded round Liza to lead her down to the sheltered bank of the creek.

"Do you remember now, Iriook?" Namoonie said proudly. "This is our winter place."

"Oh!" was all Liza could manage to say. The snow house with its tunnel entrance seemed cosier and better constructed than these tents ... if you could so call a collection of poles tied at the top, with skins draped over them. There were three of them. She could see where smoke escaped from the gap at the top where the skins did not quite meet, and

43

where the snow and wind would be bound to come in, she thought with a shiver.

Liza looked from this meagre dwelling place to the empty grey-white land that stretched out in every direction. She could feel sobs gathering in her chest, and she had to fold her arms across her front to hold the pain. The City was gone. The expedition was gone. She would never find her way back, never; for it was obvious that these primitive Ekoes wouldn't have the skill to help her. She would have to say goodbye to John, and Janet and Win and Letty, to the house Mother, to her own mother and father, to Master Bix. From this day on, this poor sad place was all she had.

She looked again at the creek, the stubby willows crowding together. She looked at the rough tents, the only man-made objects in this terrible empty land; and she looked at the faces, wide, smiling, welcoming. And she made a decision.

"It is a good place," said Iriook.

4

A good place, Liza had said, complimenting the Ekoes on their poor home. But, little by little, in scraps of conversation and explanations of things 'forgotten', she learned that this place was not really home either. Not in the same way that the City was. Namoonie stretched out his arms and turned around. "This is our home. The land."

She learned that the creek was a waiting place, one of the many through the barren lands. Any place would do that had a little wood and water, their needs were so small, so simple. What were they waiting for? She could not understand. She only knew that each day was a waiting for an expected, necessary, terribly important event.

"What is it?" she asked Namoonie again and again.

"You cannot have forgotten the caribou," he answered at last, and she had nodded wisely.

"Ah, yes. The caribou." She dared not ask any more. As long as they chose to believe that she was the missing Iriook, so long would she belong to them as daughter, sister, friend. But no longer. So she asked no more questions, but her eyes followed those of the others as they stared into the empty north.

Every day they cut holes in the ice and jigged lines until the fish rose and snapped. Liza found she was good at it, and soon she was able to smack a fish on its head with a stone and disengage the bone hook without a tremor. By the time the sun was low in the ring on the second day she had a whole row of fish freezing on the surface of the ice.

It was good to sit close together around the small fire, stripping the flesh off the fish with their fingers, stuffing it in their mouths, savouring the delicate flavour. After supper while the Northern Lights crackled overhead, they huddled under the furs and told stories until they fell asleep. Just by listening to the stories Liza understood more and more their way of speaking, and, little by little, began to speak as they did. It was a leisurely life, not paced by clocks.

When Liza spoke of the ring they could not understand why she should call it that.

"As one can see, it is not a ring. A ring goes so." Namoonie held up his hand with the forefinger and thumb touching.

"But we see only part of it. It goes all the way round."

"Round what?"

"Earth, of course." It was her turn to stare.

Namoonie smiled patiently. "As you can see, Iriook, it begins near the winter's sunrise and ends near its setting. Like an open mouth. The Mouth of Paija. Do you not remember how it all began?"

When she shook her head Kidlak retold the tale, while the small children huddled close under the furs in anticipation.

"Long ago in the beginning time, the sun shone equally all year round, and all the animals were happy, except for Caribou and Musk Ox, whose coats were so thick that they

45

were too hot. So a great shaman, a powerful man who was able to talk with the spirits who order the land, asked the tornrait if he could make life more comfortable for Caribou and Musk Ox. So the tornrait moved the sun in the sky, just a little, so that there was summer, a time of heat and light, and winter, a time when it was cold and dark. Then all the animals were happy, because they all had some of what they needed.

"All except for Wolverine. Wolverine was a mean and selfish animal, and he hated the dark and the cold. So he secretly called on Paija, Paija the dreadful spirit who stumps the world on her one great leg, her hair as black as mid-winter, her mouth filled with as many teeth as there are stars in the sky. Wolverine bribed Paija to push the sun up to the top of the sky again.

'I will give you anything you want,' crafty Wolverine promised Paija.

'I will have your children to eat,' Paija demanded and showed her terrible teeth.

'Oh, no! Take Caribou's children. Or Musk Ox's. Not *mine*,' protested Wolverine.

'I do not want Caribou's children. I do not want Musk Ox's. I want *yours*, and if you will not give me them then I will eat the sun,' Paija said crossly, and she opened her huge mouth wide, wide, and swallowed up the sun. At once it became dark and cold, colder than it had ever been, and ice began to fill up the land. Now Wolverine had even more to complain about than before, which served him right for being so selfish."

"But the sun comes out again at ringrise," Liza said. It was a lovely story, and the way Kidlak told it made it almost believable, even though it wasn't very scientific.

"You must remember, Iriook, that the animals all apolo-gized to the tornrait for Wolverine's bad behaviour, so the tornrait made Paija spit out the sun so that it could be summer again. But every winter she swallows it once more, to remind us not to be selfish like Wolverine."

46

The tornrait were the great spirits that kept the sun and the stars in their place in the sky, Liza was told. You could see and hear them in the Northern Lights. Liza had never seen this sight before leaving the City, and at first she was scared. It had begun like a sunset glow in the north, and within a blink had swelled to high pillars and swaying draperies, to arches and pinnacles, made of unearthly green light shot with flashes of hot pink. And the sky had crackled.

"It is sky music," Namoonie told her. "The tornrait are all dancing the Great Dance. It is a sign. Soon the caribou will come."

Was it just a coincidence? The very next morning a great beast, fat and sleek, its coat a shining brown, head branching like a tree, strolled down to the far side of the creek. Liza was the first to see it, and she clutched Namoonie's arm and pointed.

"Ayah! Caribou!" he whispered, and reached slowly, quietly for his bow. The great animal stood snorting, sucking in the air, suddenly disquieted by the smell of smoke from the camp. But even as its shoulder muscles twitched before flight, an arrow plunged into its neck and another into its belly.

Then Namoonie was yelling, bounding across the frozen creek and up the far slope, his knife in hand. The others appeared, carrying knives and bowls, swarming around the fallen beast.

"Iriook, fetch me the big bowl," Namoonie's mother, Nawpachee, called urgently.

When Liza got back from the tent, the snow around the caribou was churned up and pinky red. The bowl was snatched from her hands and held beneath the neck. A knife flashed. Liza shut her eyes.

When she opened them again the brimming bowl was being passed from hand to hand. Their eyes shone, their lips were edged with red, not just Agaguk and Kiawat, but gentle Kidlak and Nawpachee, and Namoonie and the children. Even little Soo. They laughed as if it were wine. When the bowl was held out to her she backed away, shaking her head. She was not enough Iriook that she could drink *that*.

They didn't argue, but left her alone and turned back to the fallen beast. They worked swiftly, neatly, cutting from neck to belly, putting the liver and heart carefully in bowls, skinning it out and quartering it.

Before the sun had moved a hand's breadth along Paija's mouth there was nothing in the ridge above the creek but a tumble of pink snow. Most of the meat was left to freeze, the skin was scraped carefully, and every piece of fat was collected and rendered down over a small fire. Then the big stew pot was set on the fire, and while they waited the family sat around it, laughing and talking.

The plate of raw liver was put on the ground in front of Namoonie, because it was he who had killed the caribou, Liza guessed. He cut a sliver from it and offered it formally to his mother.

"Oh-oh, the caribou comes. Nawpachee, Mother, eat," he sang; and she picked the slice of liver off his knife and munched it, smacking her lips, the juice running down her chin.

He offered a slice to each of the others, and to Liza. Something in the way the others watched her warned Liza that she had better not fail this test of being Iriook, and she forced the raw liver into her mouth and made herself chew and swallow it.

Namoonie looked so proud and happy that Liza even managed a sickly smile, though her stomach was churning.

That caribou buck was the forerunner. In the following days the main herd came through, at first in twos and threes, then in tens, in hundreds. The ground shook at their passing and a pungent farmyard smell filled the air. For three days the family worked without ceasing, killing, bleeding, skinning and butchering, dropping to sleep when it became too dark to see even with lamps, and then rising again, knife in hand, at the first predawn glow.

Then, equally suddenly, it was all over. The caribou had gone south and would not be seen again until after ringrise.

The frozen meat was cached under stones, the precious fat piled up in the tents like blocks of pale bricks, and a pile of furs lay ready for finishing. In due course the bones and sinews would become weapons, tools, thread. Everything they needed they had. Now they could face winter. Now, when the creek froze to the very bottom so they could no longer break the ice to fish, they would have nothing to fear.

Liza looked at her family, dirty, stained, their lips crusted with dried blood. For a second she saw them with her City eyes and was revolted. But only for a second. She was one of them now. She ate flesh with them. She had taken her place at their side with a knife. She was skilful at skinning, fast and careful, so the skins were never pierced. They were her family, and she was worthy of being one of them. Even Agaguk grumpily accepted her now. She *was* Iriook. She had to be Iriook to survive.

The cold was a clenched fist crushing the land. Even in the tents, with the grudging warmth of a tiny fire or a lamp, Iriook shivered.

"It is those spirit clothes you are wearing," Kidlak said, plucking contemptuously at the padded jacket and trousers. "There is no warmth in them. Now we have fresh skins, I will make you a new set, better than the clothes you were wearing when that Ino stole you from us."

She cut and sewed rapidly, measuring Iriook only by eye. Between one full moon and the next they were ready, and fitted perfectly. There was a set of trousers and tunic worn with the hair inward, it was explained, so that her sweat would condense on the tops of the hairs and fall away from her body so that she would not get chilled. On top of it was another suit cut more loosely, hooded and worn with the fur out. Kidlak had made a design of inlaid triangles of different coloured fur at the shoulder and around the bottom of the outer parka, the hood of which was edged with wolverine fur, that same greedy animal that had caused all the trouble with Paija long ago. There were also two pairs of boots and two sets of mittens.

Now, when she sat next to Namoonie, his arm around her,

the children at their feet like puppies, she was as warm as the others. Nawpachee and Kidlak told stories incessantly. It was a way of passing the dark cold days. Nawpachee even had a story about the loss and finding of Iriook. The children loved to hear this one.

"There were once two of the People who had six children, three boys and three girls. Every one of them was beautiful and fat and healthy, blessed by the spirits. But the most blessed was the eldest, a girl called Iriook..."

At this point in the story Iriook's younger brothers would put their hands over their mouths and giggle, and then Nawpachee would pretend to be angry and stop until they were serious again.

"One day in late winter the People travelled far towards the rising sun, farther than they had ever gone before. They were looking for the special spirit fire that would give them light and warmth, for they were running out of wood."

The spirit fire, Liza realised, was the kerosene that Tech teams had taken on their expeditions to the ice-field, and left in caches on previous trips. All that seem so far away as to be a kind of dream.

Nawpachee went on. "After four days they found the spirit·fire and loaded it on their sleds. But even though they had said all the prayers to thank the spirits for giving them the fire, this time the spirits were angry. On the second night of their journey back they made a snow house and went to sleep. In the morning they woke to find that Iriook was not there with the other children.

"When they went outside they could see her footprints, blurred by the wind. And after a little, no footprints. The People grieved and waited in the same snow·house for a full moon in case Iriook should return. Every day they searched for her and called out her name and begged the spirits to return her, but they would not. The nights were silent. The spirits did not speak. There was no Iriook! So they went away back to their own place."

Nawpachee's voice dropped. As if she were reliving the

past sorrow, Kidlak began a wordless lament, like the sad lonely sound of the wind among the willows. Liza felt a shiver run down her back. Even the brothers stopped giggling and their dark eyes were solemn. Ruthee and Soo softly took up their mother's lament. Liza felt tears running down her own cheeks and wondered why she should be crying. But it was a good feeling.

Nawpachee took up the story again. "Three times Paija swallowed the sun in her great mouth. Three times the tornrait made her spit it out again. Summer came and went, and again Paija swallowed the sun and the land began to grow dark. Again the People travelled towards the sunrise looking for spirit fire. But they would travel only three days, because to go farther would be unlucky. Alas, they found no nests containing spirit fire.

'I will go on alone,' the boy Namoonie said, the one who was to have married Iriook when she was grown."

Liza felt herself blush, and she looked under her lashes at Namoonie. But he and everyone else was listening to the story.

"Namoonie set out with one sled and a dog team towards the place where the sun rises in summer, and near the end of his journey he saw one of the nests, a long way off, brightly coloured in the snow. He prayed very hard to the spirits and kept one hand on an amulet that a powerful shaman had once given him. He stayed on the ridge and watched. Night fell and still he waited. In the morning he was still watching to see if it was safe to go closer and take the spirit fire from the nest.

"Suddenly the nest opened and out of it fell a strange creature. Namoonie was afraid at first because he thought he was seeing the Ino who had stolen Iriook. But it did not behave like an Ino but like a person whose mind has gone. So Namoonie hid the sled and team below the ridge and then ran swiftly down to the nest. When he looked inside he could see that it was half filled with spirit eggs! There was no sign of an Ino, though you can be sure that he kept one hand on his amulet all the time, in case it should suddenly appear.

"He looked around, and there, coming right out of the place where Paija's mouth gapes the widest, was a girl! He knew right away that it was Iriook, even though her face was spirit pale and she wore strange clothes. The spirits that held her fought like demons, but Namoonie overcame them and tied Iriook to the sled and took her back to the People. Little by little the memory of the time she had spent in the spirit world faded and the memory of her life as Iriook returned, though her hair remained the strange colour of the spirit nest, to remind the People of where she had been."

"Ayee!" the children chorused.

Nawpachee's voice was so hypnotic that Liza found herself wondering: which *is* the real me – Liza or Iriook? Was that other life no more than a dream of a spirit world? Yes, it had to be that, for if the other world were real she would not be able to bear this one.

Kiawat leaned forward and put a few twigs on the fire. The light flared and showed the circle of faces. Kidlak put a pot of water to heat. Soon it would be time to sleep.

"Iriook, what was it like in the spirit world?" Soo asked boldly.

"Yes, tell us," chorused the other children.

Still wrapped in the mystery of Nawpachee's story Iriook/Liza reached back, as if into the nearly forgotten past. "It was a very different world." She hesitated, trying to find words that would fit. "We lived in a square stone house inside a hill."

"Ayee!"

"As big as this tent?"

"Oh, as big as a thousand tents. There were many people, maybe two hundred families. Only we did not live close and warm like this, but apart from each other. We did not touch each other much," she remembered. "There was no hunting, no caribou. We ate food that was made right inside the hill, food made of..." How could she explain? "The food was pretend food as well as green stuff that was grown."

"No wonder you were so thin and white when you came back, you poor twig," Nawpachee said sympathetically.

"We slept in little boxes lined with cloth, separate from each other, and we washed our bodies every day in a special room where warm water came out of the ceiling."

Everyone gasped at that. Kidlak asked, "What stories and songs did you have in the dark days when the sun was in Paija's mouth?"

Iriook thought back the long, long way to Liza's life. "Why, there were no songs," she remembered. "And no real stories. Though there was music, that made me want to dance, but nobody else felt that way: They just sat with their legs as heavy as stones. It was never dark in the City. You wouldn't know it was winter, except that the windows were covered over. I remember putting up the shutters just before ... before..."

Before what? She didn't want to remember. It was safer to forget. "Yes, inside the hill there was always light, summer and winter, day and night."

"I would not like to live in the spirit world," Kiawat said, and scratched his stomach comfortably. "It is no wonder that your mind had wandered away when Namoonie found you. Ayee, what a terrible way to live!"

The water bubbled and the leaves were thrown in. The horn cup was passed around the circle. When everyone had drunk the herb tea they settled down to sleep among the warm furs. Outside the skin tent the cold night lay heavily over the land and the snow fell. Far to the north the ice sheet grew with the pressure of the new snow upon the old. Slowly it crept south.

Iriook lay with the warmth of Soo and Ruthee against stomach and back. I must be Iriook, she thought. Liza was the dream, for if I were Liza I would go mad living like this. I *am* Iriook. I have come back from the unnatural place of the spirits and I belong here.

A long way off wolves howled at the faint moon, no more than a pale circle behind the shadowing ring. The sad sound

53

echoed across the empty land. But Iriook slept and did not stir.

5

The moon waned, a small pale shape in the cavern of Paija's mouth, eaten to the sliver of a finger nail, only to grow again. Seven times the night ate the moon, and seven times it was reborn. Every day the dull copper disc that was the sun struggled slowly towards the edge of Paija's lips. It began to get a little warmer.

Even though the days lengthened, the ice on the creek was still solid. It was too thick to chop, so there were no fish. The frozen caribou meat was almost finished and there was only one small block of fat left.

The People slept for most of the day as well as through the night. They ate sparingly, only one small meal a day. They all grew thin and the faces of the children no longer shone with fat as they had when Iriook first returned.

Liza would have gone mad with impatience, with hunger, with the discomfort of always being cold, with the fear of death. Iriook learned patience from her small brothers and sisters, who never complained, no matter now meagre the daily ration of meat and fat.

Her fingers learned – but wasn't it more like relearning? – the skills of sewing a fine waterproof seam with sinew and a bone needle. She inlaid different colours of fur to make a design, and her designs were unusual and beautiful.

She listened to the stories and songs, that were history and religion and a sense of being important and belonging to each other and to the land, until it seemed that she had known them always.

"Tomorrow," Namoonie said one day. "Look at the sky." Iriook's eyes followed his pointing hand, and she saw a stripe of brilliant white across the north and at the place where the snow met the sky.

"What is it?"

"The tornrait's promise. Tomorrow the sun will escape from Paija's mouth. Tomorrow it will be summer."

"And the caribou?"

"They will return a little later. When the snow is not so deep."

Iriook licked her dry lips. She did not know what she looked like; the People had no mirrors. But she was hungry all her waking hours, and when she put her hands to her face she could feel her cheekbones sticking out like shelves. And she could count her ribs.

"There will be fish soon," Namoonie consoled her. "While we wait for the caribou."

But all Iriook could think of was a bowl of steaming blood and a slice of liver still warm from the caribou's body. She swallowed her saliva and hugged her empty stomach with her arms.

Next morning Kidlak woke them all before sunrise. She and Nawpachee took the last piece of meat, a flat slab dry and dark with frostburn, and chopped it into the shape of a big circle. Then they made a fire, not a tiny fire of willow twigs, but a blaze of roots soaked in the spirit fire that Namoonie had brought back from the nest where he had found Iriook. It burned brightly, but with a strange dark smell that stirred memories in forgotten corners of Iriook's mind. No, don't think about that, she told herself. There is no place but Here, and no time but Now.

Agaguk and Kiawat brought out their drums, and, as the light in the sky began to brighten, they began to pound on them with a steady rhythm that repeated itself over and over, slowly at first and then little by little growing faster. The sound was like the slow awakening of the giant heart of the frozen land.

The light grew brighter still. The snow flushed a glorious pink. Together Kidlak and Nawpachee laid the sun-shaped slab of meat on the fire. It began to hiss and bubble at its edges, and the smell was so wonderful that Iriook moaned softly.

"Are you listening, oh Paija?" Kidlak called politely. The drums beat on. "Take our sun-offering. This is good caribou meat, the last of the caribou meat. Give us back the sun, oh Paija, so that our days may be warm."

"Hear us, oh Paija!" Nawpachee joined in, and the children called out shrilly. Iriook found her eyes fixed on the slab of meat slowly baking, then blackening, in the flames. Was none of it to be for them?

The sun rose above the horizon, an unbearably bright silver, still half hidden by the dark arch. The white land flushed to gold.

"Ayee! Thank you, Paija!" The children jumped up and down and yelled. Kidlak and Agaguk were hugging each other, and he was actually laughing. Nawpachee and Kiawat were in each other's arms. Iriook stood with her thin face to the forgotten warmth, her eyes shut against the brilliance. Then she was picked up and whirled around in a great bear-hug against Namoonie's chest. She looked into his thin grimy face, his eyes bright and laughing, and suddenly she remembered another man, another embrace. Long ago in that other time. What was his name? But no, better not to try and remember. Memory was dangerous...

A scream tore open the sky and they all flung themselves down in the snow. Three enormous black birds appeared, as if flung from the centre of the land below the mouth of Paija. One bore away towards the sunrise, another towards its setting. The third flew directly above the creek.

The noise was appalling, like that of no earthly bird. All but Iriook buried their faces so that they should not see what was not permitted. Only Iriook saw the monstrous shadow pass over the camp and vanish into the north.

Her heart thumped and she felt the fear of her people, the terrible fear of the unknown, claw at her throat. Yet the buried part of her that was Liza said, deep inside herself, why,

56

they are only aeroplanes after all. She stared up at the empty sky while knowledge fought with fear. There was a softness like dew falling on her upturned face. Was it dew or dust? When she wiped her face and looked at her hands there was nothing to see.

Silence flooded back in, and the People scrambled to their feet and looked at each other in amazement and fear.

"Is it an answer? What do you think, Nawpachee?" Kidlak asked, and her voice trembled.

"It is Paija who sent the spirit birds, that is evident. But whether in friendship or anger, time alone will tell." Nawpachee looked down at the smouldering remains of their fire. There was nothing left but a small heart of red charcoal. "See, there is no meat left. Not a scrap. That she took our offering is a good sign. Surely she will be our friend." She covered the remains of the fire with fresh snow. The hot charcoal hissed, blackened, glistened wetly.

"It was the last of the meat, too," Soo piped up. "The very last."

"Yes indeed. It was a powerful gift."

They all nodded and began to look more cheerful in spite of their hunger. There was not even a memory of the smell of burning meat left. Nothing but a dead wet fire. Iriook felt a sudden stab of guilt. How she had *begrudged* that sacrifice! How her mouth had watered! Why, she had almost reached out and grabbed the sun-meat from the fire when it began to burn! Could *she* have spoiled the sacrifice with thoughts like that? Was it possible? Paija was great and powerful, but was she powerful enough to read what was inside a person's mind? Were the giant birds – no, aeroplanes – Paija's answer to the sacrifice? How could they be? That was nonsense. They belonged to that *other* life. She puzzled and turned these thoughts over and over in the silence of her mind.

But it was ringrise and the sun shone! Even hunger did not hurt as much when the sun warmed one's body. The grey and formless land leapt into sharp definition, a contrast of blazing white and dark blue shadows. The smallest hill, each rise of windblown snow, became important because of the depth of its shadow. Every snow grain stood out separately.

Iriook's nose burned and peeled painfully, and Kidlak smeared a little of their precious store of fat on her face. "She still has a spirit skin, poor little one," she excused the extravagance to the others.

Agaguk said nothing, but he frowned whenever he saw Iriook's sunflushed face. As much as possible she stayed out of the way of his silent anger.

The ice shrank back from the edges of the creek and a line of green appeared. Now they were able to chop through to the water beneath and jig for fish. Oh, the joy of a full stomach! The children gorged themselves without hindrance. But their elders watched the horizon beneath Paija's mouth, and their eyes were anxious and their faces lined.

"A full belly is not enough," Namoonie reminded Iriook. "We must have fat and the magic that is in fresh meat and blood. Without them we will sicken and die." His eyes turned back to the land beneath the smudgy arch. "Soon. Oh, great tornrait, send us the caribou soon!"

Several days later they were still waiting for the caribou to pass when Ottochie, the eldest of Iriook's brothers, came running into the tent. "Ayee! The snow is turning black!"

"You have sundogs in your head," his mother retorted, and went on shaking out the furs and handing them to Iriook to pile neatly around the edges of the tent.

But then Namoonie put his head inside. "It is true. The world is turning black. What can be happening?"

They ran out to look. Sure enough, the snow had changed. A layer of fine powder, like charcoal, lay across the surface of the snow for as far as they could see. It was not really black, but more like a sickly grey. It lay only on the surface. When they scooped the greyness off the top, the snow beneath was clean and white.

"Perhaps it will melt away in the sun," they said to each other. But the next day the surface of the snow was darker, as if the tiny specks of black were growing closer to each other.

58

One did not even have to wear sun-goggles, for now the snow looked even darker than it did when the sun was inside the mouth of Paija. When they pushed the dirty snow aside there was a strange smell, like dark places and rot. Iriook shuddered at it. Again memory stirred faintly, a long way down, like a great fish under a stone.

The first of the caribou appeared out of the south that day. It was a doe, winter-thin, rough coated. It pawed at the black snow beneath the creek to reach the lichens beneath. Agaguk dispatched it with a single swift arrow.

There was only a little fat around the kidneys and intestines, and it was scrupulously cut out and melted down. The liver was shared out, a very small meal; and when the stew pot was filled the rest of the meat was cut into thin strips and hung from the willow bushes to dry in the hot sun.

The stew should have been a joyous feast, the first meat after winter's long hunger. But they were all uneasy and there was little talking as they reached into the pot for their share. On all sides was the strange snow, seeming to grow blacker while they looked at it. The smell of decay was in their nostrils. They could taste it through the salty goodness of the fresh meat.

"Paija is angry," Agaguk muttered, and no one denied it. He scowled at Iriook more angrily than ever, and she began to be afraid.

Before dawn of the next day more of the caribou passed by. They were all does, heavy with young, and accompanied, many of them, by yearlings. They were a sad sight, antlerless, their coats dark and mangy, dragging tatters of their winter coats. They were allowed to stop and eat and pass on.

"Soon the bucks will come," Namoonie said, when Iriook asked him why they did not get some more meat. "Now we have eaten a little we can afford to wait. The does and the young ones are the future of the herd, as you and I and the children are the future of the People."

Iriook puzzled over the driving need of the caribou to go north before the snow had even melted from the ground.

Namoonie shrugged. "It is their way. It is said that long ago in the beginning time, before Paija swallowed the sun, the herds came this way at the same moon, but then it would have been already summer and the snow gone from the land. Perhaps the caribou have long memories and do now as they did then. Perhaps too that is why they wait until after the sun is in Paija's mouth to leave our home for the winter."

The dried meat strips were all gone from the willow bushes and into the stew pot before the first bucks arrived. They too were thin and ragged looking. But thin as they were they were food, and they were killed, though sparingly, enough for no more than a moon.

"Soon we will follow them to the summer place, where the calves will be born. They will grow fat and healthy again with the good grass and lichens of our land. Then we will be fat too," Namoonie promised.

As soon as the herd passed the tents were torn down. The skins were bundled up and the tent poles bound carefully together. Everything was dismantled smoothly and with a lack of fuss and talk that showed Iriook more clearly than words that this had been done yearly for many years.

When they set out she looked back regretfully. She had begun to feel that the creek, the willows, the sheltering low ridge, were 'home'. Once more she was to be uprooted. But she noticed that none of the others looked back, not the women, not even little Soo. They moved away as casually as if they were going for an accustomed walk.

But something was wrong. She sensed it in the frown that creased Kiawat's goodnatured face, and in the bitter twist of Agaguk's lips. The snow was melting fast, too fast. They should be able to travel easily over its surface with the heavily laden sleds. Instead, they were having to struggle with runners that were constantly clogged with wet snow. Their snowshoes sank deeply and came up covered with black slime. Each step was a labour. The dogs shivered and whined. The smell of decay was everywhere, revolting their stomachs, so that it was difficult to eat, even after a day's long journey.

Before noon on the third day the sky changed. There was a smudge like a dark cloud in its empty blueness. They struggled on, and the smudge became a flock of dark birds, rising and circling, settling on the wet snow and rising again. Before dusk they had reached the place, but by then the birds had gone. There was only the remains of a yearling caribou, nothing left but bones and hide.

"Why should it have died?" Kiawat asked. They stood in a circle around the small ugly body, all hipbones and head and empty eye sockets.

"Ask *her*!" Agaguk pointed at Iriook. His cheeks were hollow, and there was a strange light in his small dark eyes like the red spark in the heart of a piece of charcoal. His pointing hand shook. "Ask *her*. All these bad things have happened since you brought her into our tent. Ask her what she is and what she wants with us."

"She is your daughter, old man," Kidlak said sharply. The children stared, their eyes large with fear.

"You said she would change back. I see no change. She is not the daughter, Iriook, I remember. I see a white spirit skin that peels in the sun. I see pale eyes and hair the colour of the spirit nest. I see a creature of darkness, a dweller under the earth. See what she has brought us." He gestured wildly at the slimy snow and the dead caribou. "Blackness and death she brings us. Nothing but blackness and death!"

"I'm not. I didn't. Please..." Iriook's voice was almost too weak to be heard. Her heart thumped frighteningly.

"Of course not, poor little one. You are my daughter, Iriook, never fear. As for you, old man, you are mad. The black snow has turned you mad."

"Aaaaah!" With a shriek Agaguk leapt across the circle to where Iriook huddled close to Kidlak, and caught her by the neck with two powerful wiry hands.

The only thing that saved her from death was the hood of her tunic. Instead of being able to grasp her bare throat Agaguk was forced to hold her through the fur. Even so the pressure increased. Iriook struggled and felt her eyes grow dark. She choked. She couldn't breathe at all. Her knees gave, but his hands were still there, pushing her down, pushing her back into the snow that smelt of death, pushing her into blackness...

6

Liza was dreaming that she had fallen into one of the big yeast-culture vats, and that all her friends were standing around the edge laughing. There were Janet, Win, Lettie. And wasn't that John over there, laughing more loudly than all the others? She couldn't stay afloat much longer. She dog-paddled frantically and stretched out her hands.

"John, help me," she tried to say, but wasn't able to talk.

He reached out to her and she stretched up her hands, but he ignored them and put his hands round her throat.

"No!" she screamed in a silent whisper, and her mouth was filled with the bitter brew. "Master Bix!" she screamed again, and magically he was there, standing improbably balanced on the rim of the vat.

He ignored her screams for help, or perhaps he could not hear them. "Once more," he said to John. "She's not nearly dark enough yet. She must be dark enough to melt..."

And John pushed her head right under...

She woke up gasping. The horrible smell of the yeast culture was still in her nostrils and the bitter taste was in her mouth. But she wasn't in the City at all. She was lying on her back, under an open sky, a sky of deep intense blue.

That's funny, she thought, dreamily. It was ringset only a few days ago, and now it's summer again. Her eyes shut.

When she opened them again two strange women were bending over her. Their faces were kind and gentle, though very dirty, with black hair that hung forward to tangle in the draggled fur of their tunics. Fur?

Liza began to ask where she was, but when she tried to talk she could only cough. Her throat felt as if it were on fire. A little tepid water, tasting bad, was dribbled into her mouth and she managed to swallow it. Her head ached abominably. Had she hit it on something? She moved her neck and groaned. Lay still, shut her eyes and slept again.

When she woke up the pain in her throat had subsided to a sore neck, and her headache was little more than a background grumble. She opened her eyes cautiously, remembering the light that had stabbed her eyes before. But the sun had set. It was evening, and she was lying on a pile of furs in a dry rocky area that had been scraped clear of snow. A little way off there was a fire, and shadowy figures.

– I am Liza, she told herself, and I live in the City. Only I am not there now because ... because...

– Because I am Iriook also. I have been Iriook all winter, not acting, but somehow being her. How did I do it? And what am I going to do now? Can I go on? Now I know I'm Liza all the way through I'll just be play–acting ...

– But if I am *not* Iriook then Agaguk is certainly going to kill me, or at least make the others abandon me out here, which will come to the same thing. How long can I go on pretending to be Iriook without them noticing how strange I am? And *how* am I going to get back to the City?

A shadow came between her and the firelight, and she lay still with her eyes shut. Something touched her hand. "Iriook?"

It was Namoonie's voice, and she opened her eyes and looked up at him. He was no more than a shape with the fire at his back. She had no idea what he was thinking. Be careful, Liza, she told herself.

"My throat hurts." It was a safe enough remark.

"The black snow drove your father mad."

"Is he all right now? Where is he? Namoonie, I am afraid."

"Don't be. I will protect you."

"Promise?" Liza asked cunningly. If she could just get him on *her* side.

"What do you mean – promise? I have said it, have I not?" His voice was stiff, offended.

Liza bit her lip. That had been the wrong move. Yet Namoonie was her only hope of escape. How was she to get him to help her? He was so different from the boys in the City. She couldn't play games with him, twist him around her thumb. It wouldn't work that way, the way it had with John...

Yet Namoonie was a much better person than John, a better person than anybody she knew, much better than herself. And she was glad that he was that way. Only if she couldn't *use* him to help her to get back to the City, what *was* she going to do?

She sat up cautiously. She hurt all over, but the aches were bearable. "Where is Agaguk now?" she whispered, looking around.

"He and Kiawat have gone ahead with one of the sleds. They want to get closer to the caribou. Perhaps that young one died because it was sick. Perhaps it had nothing to do with the black snow."

"But you think it did, don't you?"

"You have only to smell it. It smells of death. Also it melts too fast, faster than snow has ever melted before."

"Do you think it comes from the spirit world?"

"Where else? The question is, why? Are the spirits angry with us for something we have done, or have failed to do? Or are they fighting with each other, and it is just bad luck that we and the caribou are in the way? If they would only tell us we would not be so uneasy. It is the not knowing..."

Liza did not answer. A marvellous, stupendous idea had just sprung into her brain, the best idea she had ever had. A safe way of getting back to the City! She went over it carefully, step by step. There wasn't a flaw in it anywhere. She stared at the shadows beyond the fire with unfocused eyes. She didn't answer when Namoonie spoke to her again. She would have to act. Could she put on such a performance? Well, she must, that's all there was to it. Her life depended on it.

Namoonie was shouting her name. Now she deliberately ignored him. She heard him call out to Kidlak and Nawpachee. They ran up to where she was sitting. And the children. They all stood around the place where she sat and stared. She kept motionless, her eyes unfocused, gazing into the distant shadows.

"Ayee! Where is she?" Soo whispered. It was hard not to smile, harder still not to hold out her arms and comfort the little girl. Liza kept her body rigid and tried not to listen to them. Their voices were like mosquitoes buzzing.

"She has gone to the spirit world again," Namoonie said. "We were talking and then suddenly she was gone."

"Perhaps Agaguk was right all along. Perhaps she belongs to an Ino and it was all a trick." Nawpachee's voice quivered. Liza dug her nails into the palms of her hands. Dear good Nawpachee, who was kind and clever and wouldn't hurt a fly.

"No! She is Iriook. I am sure she is Iriook. How could I be mistaken in that?" Kidlak's voice trembled also, but not with fear, or at least not just with fear of the spirits, but with fear of losing again the daughter she had lost before.

What will she do when I have left? Liza thought. What can I do to make it up to her? Then she pushed the thoughts out of her mind. She forced herself to sit upright, motionless, her eyes staring unblinkingly through the people who had for so many months been friend and family, more family than she had ever found in the City. For an instant her resolution weakened, as she thought about their love. They had saved her life. They had cared...

But it's all a lie. I don't belong to them. I'm not Iriook. I could never really be Iriook, could I? Not for ever...

She sat and stared until her eyes began to water and the muscles of her cheek and neck began to twitch and quiver. Only then did she allow herself to blink, to sigh and stretch, to focus on the anxious faces around her.

"You were on a journey, cousin?" Namoonie spoke formally.

"Yes." Her voice sounded stiff and her lips moved as if she

had forgotten how to use them. But that was all right – that is how she would sound if she were really coming back from the spirit world. "A long journey. Back to the place where I was taken before."

"Ayee!"

"But this time you came back by yourself!"

"That is good, very good, Iriook."

Liza shook her head slowly and looked sad. It wasn't difficult to look sad, deceiving them as she was. "I have a message for you. And then..." She put her face in her hands and sobbed, only pretend sobs; deep inside her a heaviness grew like a cold stone.

"Don't cry." Namoonie stroked her tangled red hair. "Tell us what happened." His big hand was very gentle. She could hardly bear to go on.

"No, I must wait for the men to return. I will tell all of you together. Then you must decide for yourselves what is to be done." After that she would say no more, but sat apart from them; and when the stew pot was taken off the fire she would not eat, even though her stomach ached with emptiness.

Liza did not sleep well that night. Perhaps it was hunger. Perhaps it was the thought of the plan that kept her awake. It seemed that the tent was at the same time chilly and stuffy. The family crowded so closely about her that she could feel their breathing, hear every movement, the snoring, the turning, the muttering.

The smell of meat and rancid fat was everywhere, on skin and clothes and hair and fur. Everywhere. It was strange that she hadn't been aware of it before, or at least not for a long time.

The men arrived back in the dusk between sunset and sunrise that was the summer arctic night. Liza alone was still awake to hear their voices and the sound of the dogs. She lay and thought, thoughts that stretched like thin pale threads back into her past, into the City, into what she had done to other people's lives because of that one mad idea to stow away with the expedition. Into what she had done to Kidlak, and to Namoonie who loved her.

In the morning a small fire was made as usual and a hot drink was brewed and passed around from mouth to mouth as it always was. Liza felt she could hardly bear to let her lips touch the greasy cup. But it was necessary. Agaguk was watching her. It seemed that now he was always watching her. She managed to keep her face expressionless as she sipped and passed the cup on.

When they had finished drinking, Agaguk still stared at her. What was he thinking? She stared right back at him, trying not to show her fear. "I had a dream yesterday," she challenged him.

"So? Dreams are as common as mosquitoes in summer."

"This was different. I was awake."

"That is so, uncle," Namoonie added.

"It was a spirit dream," Kidlak put in.

Liza stared as calmly as she could at Agaguk, though inside she was trembling. He had such a closed face. She could not even guess at his thoughts. His eyes were almost shut and she could not tell if they still held that mad red spark. One day he will kill me, she realised. If I don't get away. One day...

She lifted her chin and spoke. "In my dream I was raised up and taken by the wind to the place inside the Hill where the Ino kept me a prisoner before. At first I was afraid and very sad, but then a voice spoke to me. It told me not to be afraid, that Paija was pleased with your offering of caribou meat. The voice told me that if I were to make the journey back to the Hill, not just in the spirit, but in the body, Paija would tell me the secret of the black snow."

Agaguk's eyes were fixed on her face. She looked calmly back. It was a duel between the spirits of the Eko man and the Tech girl. I have the advantage, Liza told herself, when she felt that her eyes might waver. Agaguk knows only his reality, but I know both mine and his. I *must* win. She kept her gaze steady, while she sat straight and still, as though completely relaxed, her hands softly in her lap.

No one spoke or moved. The breeze dropped suddenly and the flies swarmed in, crawling and biting. Still Liza refused to budge, though her hands itched to scrub away the vile insects from her eyes and nose and mouth.

"The secret of the black snow." Agaguk spoke at last, his voice like a dead willow creaking in the wind. "And why would Paija help us like that?"

"We have always honoured her, husband," Kidlak interrupted timidly.

"That is true." Agaguk nodded and stared down into the fire, deep in thought.

Thankfully Liza allowed her eyes to move away from his face. She watched the small flames darting through the willow twigs and the smoke rising straight from the green wood. Perspiration ran down her forehead, mingling with the blood of insect bites. She forced herself to ignore it.

"It is good that Paija wishes to help us, and that she asks you to go back," Agaguk went on. Kidlak made a movement towards her daughter, but Agaguk held up a hand, and at once she crouched down by the fire. "The black snow is poisonous," he went on as if she had not interrupted. "We have found more young calves sick and two that were already dead. The land smells of death. If it is necessary that our daughter go back to that place in order to shut death back into its own land, before it destroys all of us, then it must be so."

It was the first time he had called Liza 'daughter', and in that word alone was a small victory. It was the only one. In the silence Kidlak sobbed. Liza bit her lip. Everything was going splendidly, just as she had planned. She had not understood that it would be so hard to do.

"Don't cry, Kidlak." Namoonie put his capable hand over his aunt's. "All will be well. I myself will go with Iriook and see her safely to that place. And I will not leave until I can bring her back to you."

Liza opened her mouth to protest. Then she shut it again. Perhaps it wasn't such a bad idea. She would certainly need Namoonie's skill to help her find her way back to the City. Only what was she going to do with him when she was safely back home? Well, she would just have to worry about that later. One thing at a time.

She lifted her eyes from the fire and looked directly at Agaguk. "It is good and pleasing to Paija, Father," she told him firmly. "I shall go at once and Namoonie shall go with me."

7

Namoonie and Liza walked south towards high summer. It took them many days, days of hard slogging through melting putrid snow, and more days ankle deep in peaty brown muskeg. Liza sometimes wondered if Namoonie really had any clear idea of where he was going. He did not travel as she would have done, in a straight line following a compass bearing like a line drawn on a map. Instead he continually moved to east or west, taking the driest way, the smoothest path.

Perhaps he had inside him something like the inertial navigational system of the City sleds and crawlers. Perhaps his brain tallied the jogs to right or left and compensated for them, so that he never lost sight of their true heading, without him having to think about it at all.

Or perhaps it was all guesswork, and really they were lost in this primitive empty land . . .

They left behind the tainted snow and with it the smell of death and decay. They entered a world of water, of thousands of streams and freshets, a clamour of water after the silence of winter. There was colour too, moss so green that it dazzled the eyes, and a thousand varieties of flowers, the largest no bigger than her little fingernail, supported on hair-thin stems.

It was also a world of blackfly and mosquito. As the blazing sun warmed the wet moss it shivered with silvery larvae, which turned overnight into a dark cloud of aggravation and pain. Only when the wind freshened and when the noon sun baked the land were they free of it. This was the time they chose to rest and eat and talk, when they could open their mouths without the insects crawling in.

Kidlak and Nawpachee had shared with them the last of the sun-dried spring caribou meat and some scraps of fat. Though they supplemented this meagre diet with fish, they were always hungry. Further south they came upon some early strawberries. Never in her life had Liza tasted anything to compare with the sharp winy juice of those first berries.

Day after day they walked south. The nights were spent in fitful sleep, broken by the whine of blood-seeking insects. Liza dreamed often that she was walking across a flat never-ending plain. Her aching calves and thighs would twitch with her dream-walk and jerk her awake; and she would have to rub away the cramping knots in her legs before she could sleep again.

She became more aware of Namoonie each day. Winter had stripped the puppy-fat from him and now he was a man, lean and dark-skinned. In the terrifying quiet of night, lying under a caribou fur, she felt an agonizing loneliness that she had no words for. She would have liked to reach out to him, but she could not. It was as if an invisible barrier was growing between them. The further south they walked the more silent he became.

"This is the place." Namoonie's voice startled her, breaking into the silence of a morning that had started out like every other morning.

Liza stopped her mindless walk and looked around. Low rolling hills, no more than wrinkles in the land, limited their view to a kilometre or so in every direction. The land here was stony and treeless.

"What place?" Her voice sounded creaky and unused. She licked her dry lips. How long had they walked? For how many days? Where were they going? She had almost forgotten. The walking itself had become a way of life.

"Where I found you in the spirit nest, Iriook. You must remember the place."

Spirit nest? Oh, he meant the sled. Liza pulled herself

70

together. "Oh, yes, Namoonie. I remember. I came back and thought you were a bear."

"Ayee, how you fought! I had to tie you down before the spirits would leave you and let me take you to the People."

"This is the place?"

"Surely."

"How can you tell? It was knee deep in snow then. And where is the sled – I mean the spirit nest?"

"Who can tell the way of spirit things?" Namoonie shrugged. "But this is where I found you. Now *you* must remember the place the spirits brought you from. Now you must lead us."

Liza stared blankly at his lean brown face. He was counting on *her*? She had no idea. The only indication was the ring, a sombre charcoal arch scrawled across the summer sky. "That way." She pointed vaguely towards its centre and tried to remember. It all seemed a very long time ago. "We travelled from sunrise through a day and a night. Yes, and then part of the next day."

"As fast as a dog team?"

"Oh, faster than that."

"As fast as the spirit thunder birds?"

"Not *that* fast."

Namoonie nodded. "We will walk for another moon perhaps," he said matter-of-factly.

"I ... I'm not sure that I'll know the place," Liza stammered. She had a sick vision of the two of them walking on and on across this sparse world, always just missing by an hour, by a kilometre, contact with other human beings. She licked her lips. They were dry and cracked with the wind, and she felt very old, and tired down to the centre of her being.

Namoonie glanced at her and then looked quickly away. "Do not be afraid. I will not let them keep you a prisoner. We will take the secret of the black snow from the spirits. Then we will leave and go home. I promise you, I, Namoonie."

Home ... what *was* home? Was it Kidlak, Nawpachee, the

children? Or was it Win, Lettie and Janet? Master Bix? John . . . ?

They walked on south through the waning and the waxing of the moon. They walked faster now, over rocks and dry wiry grass. They were no longer plagued by flies, but on several occasions they had to go out of their way to find fresh water. Water, that had covered the melting northland, was in short supply here among the stones.

Namoonie had an instinct for finding water too. Time after time he would look around, sniff and point. "That way." And when they had gone 'that way' they would invariably come upon a creek, hidden between the ancient low hills, its willows green with the promise of water.

One morning they were making a detour towards some hidden creek and crested a low rise to see a strange sight ahead of them. Up until now all the trees had been in full leaf, hidden down in the folds of the ground where their roots might find nourishment. But now, ahead of them, there stood four strange trees on the crest of a low hill. They were leafless and were twisted into unnatural tortured shapes, perhaps by the wind.

As they stared, a cloud slipped from in front of the sun and the sudden light flared brilliantly off the silvery bark, so that they had to close their eyes. It was like the sun's reflection off metal, Liza thought. Off metal? Yes, off metal!

A warmth spread through Liza's body, a fire licking down tired back and legs. She turned to Namoonie, smiling, laughing. "The solar collectors! The windmills! We've done it, Namoonie. We're here. We're *home*!"

She caught his hand and began to run towards the low hill. He pulled back. His weight was too much for her, so she let go and went on running. Her legs were tired and heavy, her feet like lumps of dough. She tripped over a tuft of wiry grass, and before she could scramble to her feet Namoonie had caught up with her.

He pulled her to her feet and held her tight against his chest. She could feel his fingers biting into the tender muscles

72

of her upper arm right through the fur of her summer tunic.

"Let me go, Namoonie. It's all right. Don't you understand? I'm *home*."

He shook his head. "Home is back *there*. This is a trap, Iriook. The spirits will swallow you up inside the hill and I will never see you again. I will not let you go."

"It's not like that, Namoonie. Oh, I can't explain it all now, but I do live there, in the City. It is my home."

"You are Iriook, and your home is with me, back there." He turned her around, so that she faced back the way they had come. His fingers hurt her arms. "Look at your land, Iriook, the land of the People. Look well. Do not forget."

"I am not forgetting. I am Liza, not Iriook. Oh, Namoonie, let me go. Nothing bad will happen, I promise you. Let me *go*!"

She tore herself from his arms and began to run again, up the side of the Hill towards the Winter Door. It should be open on a warm day like this, to let air circulate through the City. Above her head the collectors flashed in the sun, spinning wind and sun into electricity. Now she was close enough to hear them, the steady click-click as their shafts engaged with the generators set snugly within the Hill.

Her legs would hardly move. It was like trying to run in a nightmare. She could hear Namoonie's breath harsh behind her, close behind her. His hand reached to her shoulder...

It was all right. She was at the opening, the dark hole that shafted down into the depths of the Hill. She pelted down the sloping road that led to the basement storage area where her adventure had started almost a year ago.

When she reached the cool stone-smelling storeroom she stopped and leaned against the wall, panting, her hand to her side. She looked back. Namoonie was no longer following her. There was nothing between her and the small oblong patch of light at the top of the passage.

She hesitated. Should she go back and *make* him come with her? But she knew in her heart that she could never make

73

Namoonie do anything he didn't want to. And he was stronger than she was by far. He might stop her returning. A sudden pain twisted inside her. Oh, Namoonie!

She pushed the pain away. What was the matter with her? She was home! She ran across the echoing room and up the stairs to the door at the top where John had kissed her. She pushed open the door.

"Hey, everyone, I'm back!" she yelled joyfully, and then, without knowing why, she began to cry.

In later years, when she told the story to her own children, Liza would say that she couldn't have picked a more spectacular moment for her sensational reappearance if she had staged it deliberately. The clock above the Summer Door said 'thirteen hundred'. The midday meal was just over and the population of the City was leaving the dining room.

Win's was the first face that Liza recognised and she rushed up to her with outstretched hands. "Oh, Win, I'm so *glad* to see you again."

Win let out a piercing scream that froze everyone else in the hall. Then she stiffened, her eyes rolled up and she slumped to the floor. Those who were still in the dining room rushed out at the sound of the scream, to see one of their girls unconscious on the floor, while a filthy tangle-haired Eko, dressed in dirty animal skins, stood menacingly over her.

It was fortunate, as Liza reminisced in future years, that the City Techs did not carry weapons, or the story would have ended there and then. As it was, she was grabbed by so many people at once that she was afraid she was going to be torn apart.

Her tears dried up and she shouted frantically, "It's me, Liza. Don't you recognize me? It's *me*!" But since everyone else was shouting, directions, suggestions, or simply in pure fright and anger, her voice was drowned.

"What in the name of sanity is going on?" The voice was as soft as a spider's thread, but it cut through the babble as if it were made of hot wire.

In the sudden silence Liza was able to make herself heard. "Oh, Master Bix, I'm so glad to see you. Please make them let me go. It's *me*. Liza Monroe."

Voices were raised again, as everyone began to argue that she was nothing like poor naughty, lost Liza. Win came out of her faint, caught sight of Liza again and went into noisy hysterics.

Master Bix ignored the uproar. He peered over his glasses. "Blue eyes, red hair – I think. Well, you're certainly not an Eko, whoever you are. Two of you ... You, Mary ... yes, and Annabel. Take her away and scrub her. Get rid of those clothes. No, on second thoughts have them fumigated and sent to my office. And the girl. In my office. Clean and dry and decently clothed."

He stalked off to his room. Mary and Annabel came reluctantly forward, and prodded Liza in the direction of the showers.

"Ow! You don't have to do that. I'm going."

Standing in the shower stall with hot water pouring over her head, Liza felt the last of Iriook wash off her and slide down the floor drain with the water and shampoo foam. She washed and rinsed her hair and washed it again. Wrapped in towels, she brushed her teeth fiercely, brushing away the memory of blood and raw meat and fish. Her nails were torn and jagged and she cut them as short as she could, ashamed at the women's eyes on her hands.

How smooth and soft the summer uniform was against her clean skin. How easy it was to move, how light the house sandals. She'd lost an awful lot of weight. Her ribs showed through her skin, and even when she was dressed you could see where her hip-bones protruded. Annabel clicked her tongue at the sight, and made Liza sit down, while she quite gently tried to comb the tangles out of her red hair.

"Once you have eaten and rested you must have this cut. You look like a savage."

Like a savage. But on her way to Master Bix's office no

one noticed Liza. Her uniform was identical with everyone else's. She was part of the City again, like a bee in its hive, like an ant in its colony.

Where are you, Namoonie? I can't let you go just like this . . .

In Master Bix's office she answered his many questions, and told him briefly all she could remember of what had happened to her in the ten months she had been missing, the ten months when she had been inside the skin of that other girl, the Eko girl. Namoonie's girl.

A knock at the door heralded the arrival of a tray, neatly laid with knife, fork, spoon, folded napkin. There was a cup of soup and a plate of hi-pro patties and vegetables. A fragrant smell wafted over to Liza, and with only a glance at Master Bix for permission she snatched the cup of soup and drained it.

She blushed when she saw his eyes watching her. Oh, what dreadful manners! What would he think? She shook out the folds of the napkin with careful trembling hands, laid it on her knee, and cut a small precise square from one of the patties, speared it on the fork and put it neatly in her mouth.

Her stomach ached with emptiness and saliva filled her mouth. She swallowed. Oh, Namoonie! She cut another piece of patty, carried it to her mouth, hesitated. The tears suddenly gushed from her eyes and she put down her fork and hid her blubbering face in her napkin.

"What is the matter, Liza?" Master Bix's voice was kind.

"Namoonie," she sobbed. "He's outside somewhere. Twice he's saved my life. Now he's somewhere out there alone and he's every bit as hungry as I am." She put her head down on the table. Master Bix thoughtfully moved the tray out of the way of her hair.

He let her cry for a minute, and then, when the storm had subsided, he said, "He is here, in the City. No, don't worry. He's fine. You may see him as soon as you've finished your meal."

Here? In the City? Liza's eyes shone. She blew her nose, sat up straight and ate the rest of her meal as quickly as good manners would permit. She polished the plate with her last piece of roll and then looked up to see Master Bix's eyes on her. She blushed again.

"I'm finished now, sir. May I see him?"

How strange it was to think of seeing Namoonie in this setting. How would he like her home? She longed to show him all the marvels of the City. But she hoped he wouldn't change, that he would go on being the familiar Namoonie that she knew.

"This Namoonie of yours – is he all you're thinking of?"

Liza blushed even more deeply, began to stammer reasons, got tangled up in her own words and fell silent.

"You've been gone for almost a year. We thought you were dead."

"I know. I'm sorry." Where are you, Namoonie?

"You were much mourned."

Her head came up at that and she stared. "Mourned? Me?"

"You." His soft voice reproved her. "Do you think that you can vanish out of people's lives and not affect them by your absence? Life isn't so simple, Liza."

Kidlak. Nawpachee. The children ... But how did Master Bix know that?

"Your father and mother." He spoke gently, but there was iron in his voice. "John. Even your room-mates, your floor Mother, your work crew."

She stared at him. Mother? Father? They had cared? "I didn't know," she stammered. "I thought everyone despised me."

"Why would you imagine that?"

"It wasn't imagination, sir. Truly. People *didn't* like me. I was different, I was untidy, I kept getting into trouble." She remembered taking Letty's best hair-ribbon. "I was horrible," she added. "I deserved it."

"John loved you. Did you know that?"

John. "I used him," she confessed. "Just to get away. He must absolutely hate me now."

"Nonsense." Master Bix smiled. Liza felt a sudden panic as if fences, like bars, were springing up all round her. She wasn't ready to face John. Or her parents. It was all too complicated.

Master Bix was a wise man. He looked at her in silence, and then stood up. "Come. I'll take you to your friend. But afterwards you are going to have to face your father and mother and John. Make your peace with them honestly. Don't be ashamed to tell them what you feel."

He took her through back corridors to the research section. In one of the rooms Namoonie lay on his back on a table. The ceiling lights were focused on him so that he lay in a pool of hard white light. He didn't move.

"What have you done?" Liza screamed. "He's not ... dead?" She caught his hand. It was warm, but when she let it go it flopped limply to the table. She shook his shoulders and called his name. His head rolled to one side.

She turned to the white-coated technicians who had turned from the table at the entry of Master Bix. "What have you done to him? Have you killed him? If you've..." Her fingers crooked into claws.

Master Bix caught her wrists and drove them down. "Liza, he is sleeping."

"That's no sleep," she spat angrily back, manners forgotten.

"Only a tranquillizer. He was found lurking near the Winter Door. At first they thought he was a wild animal. Only after tranquillizing him did they realise he was human. There's no harm done, I promise."

"You sure he's all right."

"I'm sure."

"Then why's he in this room, on this table. He should be in bed."

"Come, Liza. This is the first opportunity we have ever had of examining an Eko. It's an opportunity we can't miss. Don't be afraid, we won't hurt your friend. The doctors are only interested in checking his blood type, his cholesterol level, his metabolic rate – things like that. It's for the good of the whole world, you realise, to find out how the human body really responds to a cold environment. He won't be harmed. As soon as he wakes we'll see that he gets a good meal and a shower and a change of clothes."

Liza hesitated. Still holding her hands, Master Bix drew her from the room. "You can see him again as soon as he's been cleaned up."

Cleaned up. She could hear the distaste in his voice. For a moment, before the door swung shut, she saw Namoonie as he must appear to the Techs, a bundle of dirty fur, with tangled hair, torn fingernails, hands encrusted with dirt...

I looked like that too, she thought, and looked down at her clean short nails. I lived that way too, not washing, drinking blood ... like an animal.

It was in this humble mood that Liza saw her parents again ... and then John. From Mother she got a cool kiss on the cheek, from her father a pat on the shoulder. When she apologized they didn't scold her at all. They were very civilized...

It was more difficult to face John. When she thought of him and Namoonie together he became very unimportant. But he was a person who had cared for her, and she had treated him very badly. She worried about how she was going to apologize without making him feel even worse. But in the end it was an anticlimax.

They met in the hall, stopped and looked at each other in silence.

"I'm very glad you're safe," he said after a while. "You look very thin. Are you all right?"

"Yes, thanks. *You* look great. Really." It was true. He seemed more assured, more together.

There seemed to be nothing more to say except for the unsayable. "I'm sorry," Liza muttered, praying that he wouldn't make an issue out of it.

"That's okay." He did understand. "It was tough at first,

when I found out what you'd done. I felt very bitter, but how could I be angry with you when you were dead?"

"Oh, John . . ."

"It's perfectly all right now." He smiled, and then *he* looked awkward. "I hope you don't mind too much. You see . . . we all thought you were dead . . . so, me and Win . . ."

A whole mixture of feelings swamped Liza. Jealousy, a little. Win? A sense of being let-down. Relief. An awful longing to burst out laughing. John and Win. Well!

Good manners won out. She gave John a hug and a smile. "I'm glad. I truly hope you will both be very happy."

Eventually she would have to face everybody with apologies and explanations, however lame. Now she was thankful when she was told to report to the hospital for a physical, and then was sent to bed without having to face everyone at dinner.

"The bed in your old room has been taken," the nurse on duty said briskly. "You'll have to make new arrangements. For the time being you may have a bed here. We're not crowded."

So when the health scan was finished, and she had had supper alone on a tray, Liza lay in a cold clean bed in a small white room in the hospital wing. She felt cold and lonely. Had she expected anything else? More of a welcome from parents and room-mates? After all, it was not every day that one came back from the dead.

She had had a cool kiss from Mother, a few words from Father. John was fine. She should be glad of that. But she felt so flat. It seemed that after she had left the City everyone had just moved over and filled in the space she had occupied. Was that all the importance she had for any of them?

Yet Master Bix had said that she *was* missed. But you could never guess it. When Iriook vanished she was missed and mourned and made into a story to be told by the People for ever. When she had returned – it seemed to them – from the dead, she was kissed and hugged and loved. Liza. Iriook. Were there perhaps different kinds of love? Or just different ways of showing it?

She shivered. The room was very clean and white. She couldn't even smell her own body any more. She pictured herself back in the big tent, tucked in comfortably among the pungent furs, with the warmth of Ruthee at her back, her arms around the cosy Soo.

At last she managed to get to sleep. Then it seemed only a moment before she was being shaken awake. Oh, dear, she was so very tired. What could be important enough to wake a person in the middle of the night?

"Are the caribou coming?" She sat up with a jerk, and then stared at the nurse who had just wakened her.

She stared back. "What? Get up, child. Master Bix wishes to see you right away."

Liza scrambled out of bed and into her clothes.

"No, don't go until you've combed your hair. My goodness, how crumpled you are! You forgot to hang your uniform up, didn't you?"

She ran along the corridor to the main hall. To the left to Master Bix's office. The door was closed. She knocked and waited to be admitted.

It opened to a shambles. She gasped. The office of the head of the City had never looked like this before. Chairs were overturned. Papers littered the floor. A micro-fiche cabinet lay on its side, its drawers spewing out their precious content.

The room was crowded. There were three research technicians, one of them collapsed in a chair with Master Bix standing over him. The other two had their backs to the door. They were holding chairs, the legs braced in front of them like weapons. They didn't look round when Liza came in. Their eyes were glued to the figure in the far corner...

"Namoonie!" Liza gave a scream and pushed past the technicians. Master Bix caught her arm. "Be careful."

"What do you mean? He's my friend."

"I doubt it. Not now. Hold on a minute. As for you, Arthur," he said to the technician who sat white-faced in the chair. "You'd better go along to the hospital and have those wounds dressed. Anti-tetanus and antibiotics, please. The

81

human bite can be quite dangerous, I understand. And his nails were filthy. Who knows what microbes..."

The technician shuddered and staggered from the room.

Liza stared. Bites? Scratches? She walked slowly past the men with the chairs. "Namoonie, it's me."

The man in the corner of the room bared his teeth at her. Was it really Namoonie? They'd stripped off his furs and put him in standard work overalls. He looked so different from Tech people, even in their clothes. He was much darker, more squat and muscular. Now that he had lost his natural layer of fat his cheekbones protruded, giving him an animal quality. His teeth were bared in a snarl, angry or frightened, she couldn't tell. He looked more like a hungry wolf than a human.

"Namoonie, it is Iriook," Liza said. "Everything is all right, I promise you." She daren't go any closer. His eyes had the same red fire in them that Agaguk's had had.

He recognised her but his expression did not change. "It is evident that the *inua* have bewitched you and turned you into one of themselves."

"No, truly not. This is not a magic place, and these people are not spirits. They are men just as you are. Did you not see that one bleed when you bit him? They are not spirits, they are Techs, that is all."

"Not inua?" The red flame died from Namoonie's eyes.

"Truly not."

"And you?"

"I am human also."

"I saw you with my own eyes vanish into the hillside. How can a human do that?"

"The City is like a big cave, Namoonie, built right inside the hill, to keep us warm in winter, the way your snow house keeps you warm. I just went into the tunnel, like the tunnel of your snow house."

Namoonie thought. Then he shook his head. "They pricked me with a magic dart, so that all the strength went out of my arms and legs. When I woke I was dressed like this, and in this spirit place."

82

"A City. Not magic. Only science, Namoonie."

"There was a box with hot rain coming out of the top. Who ever heard of rain that can be turned on and off? Steaming, like muskeg in summer."

"Only a shower. We use them every day to keep ourselves clean."

"Every day? I see now why your skins are so pale. All the colour must wash away!"

His voice was calmer now. He relaxed and began to look around the room curiously. Liza motioned to the Techs to put down the chairs, and when they had done so she pushed Namoonie into one, and sat down facing him.

He looked at her and sighed. "You cannot be Iriook. You do not smell like Iriook."

She couldn't help smiling. His words were so much an echo of her earlier thoughts. If *she* felt uncomfortable, how much worse it must be for him. "You don't smell like Namoonie, but I know you are. And truly I am the same person who lived with you and hunted the caribou and walked halfway across the barren lands with you."

He sighed. "I don't understand."

"It'll be all right. You're tired, that's all. You must eat and then sleep. Then you will see. Everything will seem better."

At first Namoonie wouldn't touch the food that Master Bix ordered, saying it was spirit food, not fit for humans. But Liza ate and drank while he watched her, and after a time hunger overcame fear. He would not touch the knife and fork, but ate everything with his fingers. By the time the tray was empty Master Bix's desk was splattered with crumbs and gravy.

Liza blushed for him, and wondered what Master Bix must be thinking. He looked very strange in Tech uniform. To find one big enough for his shoulders they had had to pick a large size and turn back the cuffs and trouser bottoms. He looked odd, even ungainly, not at all the way he was in his own properly fitted fur tunic and trousers.

She stared at him, happy to see him again, but not knowing quite what to say. He looked at her as if she too was

83

a stranger. Then he broke the silence with an enormous yawn and a belch.

"It is time for sleep, Namoonie. Let me show you the place where you may sleep."

"Do we not all sleep together?"

Liza tried to avoid Master Bix's scandalized look. "We each have a room here. Like separate places in a big snow house," she tried to explain.

"But it is still light."

"It is night outside. In the City there are always lights. People are sleeping now, and your room can be made dark. You will sleep."

He got up reluctantly and went with her to the door. But there he balked. Whether he was afraid of the sheer size of the halls and corridors she did not know; but he bolted back inside and pressed his body against the far wall.

"Oh, dear. What are we to do? No, please don't force him to go. That will only make him worse. I suppose he couldn't ... well ... sleep *here*?" She looked pleadingly at Master Bix.

He sighed and looked around at the disaster that had once been an orderly office. "First an arena, then a picnic spot ... why not a bedroom? It's going to take days to clean up anyway. Very well, girl. He may sleep here."

"Perhaps ..." She hesitated, and then, at the twinkle in his eye, went on boldly. "Perhaps he could have his furs back. He will feel more at home."

"It shall be done." He lifted the phone from the floor. "And we'll have a guard on the door."

Liza opened her mouth to protest, but at the firm set of his lips she shut it again. When the furs arrived she spread them on the floor. "See, Namoonie. You'll sleep comfortably here. And there is a bathroom next door. Look. You won't even have to go outside."

He crawled shivering between the furs. "Stay," he pleaded.

"No." Master Bix intervened. "She must come with me. She has work to do. You will see her when you have slept. You have my word."

Liza could hardly bear the look in his eyes. She was hustled out of the room and the door firmly shut. "Why?" she asked reproachfully. "I could just as well have stayed. He was scared to death, couldn't you see?"

"I certainly could. And I'm curious to know why. And I need the answers to many other questions, such as how you managed to persuade him to bring you home now, but not ten months ago. Liza, *why* did you not come back before?"

⑧

Liza felt guilty colour flood up into her thin face. "But . . . but I couldn't," she stammered. "How could I plan to escape when I was Iriook?"

"You mean pretending to be Iriook, don't you?"

Liza shook her head. "No, sir, it wasn't like that. Oh, I'm all muddled up."

Master Bix looked at her with a calm and kindly face. "Take your time."

Liza struggled to understand herself and put what she felt into words. "At first I *had* to be Iriook, because if I wasn't then Agaguk wouldn't have let me stay, and I'd have died out there in the snow. Then . . ."

"Go on."

"It became real. I know that sounds stupid, sir, but it's true. They made me believe myself. I was one of them. They loved me – Kidlak and Ruthee and Soo and Nawpachee. And my little brothers and cousins. And . . . and everyone," she finished lamely and blushed again.

"But what was so strong in their love that it made you forget yourself, your upbringing, everything? After all, you experienced love and security here in the City. Your mother and father loved you. They mourned your loss excessively."

Liza felt again her mother's cool lips on her cheek, her

father's hand on her shoulder, his few gruff words of greeting. "I don't believe it," she blurted out.

Master Bix raised an eyebrow. "His grief interfered with your father's work for weeks."

"Well, you'd never have guessed," she muttered. Her throat felt thick and tight and she hoped she wasn't going to cry.

As if he knew how she felt he said, "We're Techs, not Ekoes. We do not parade our emotions, but that is not to say that we do not have them."

But how is one to know that one is loved? Liza thought. She could feel the comfort of Namoonie's arm around her, the warmth of Ruthee and Soo, see the laughing faces and hear the kind voices of Kidlak and Nawpachee. "They made me feel wanted, for the first time. *Me*," she burst out. "And I stayed. It was so easy to pretend to be Iriook. Then once I got used to the way of talking and living I became Iriook. I pushed Liza to the back of my mind and I forgot all about her."

"Wasn't that very difficult?"

"No, it was easy."

"So you don't like Liza Monroe very much?"

"Well, who does?" She tried to laugh, but her mouth went all crooked.

"Oh, my dear!" His voice held an unexpected compassion, and Tech or not, Liza began to cry. He handed her a handkerchief and waited patiently until the storm was over.

"I'm sorry." She scrubbed her eyes with the damp wad of cloth.

"It is I who am sorry. I can see that the City has failed you, and we have blamed our failure on you. I am sorry we have hurt you so, and I am concerned. Are there other children growing up here who feel as you do, but are not strong enough and bold enough to fight for their own survival?"

"I ... I don't know, sir." The world turned upside down. Master Bix at a loss, asking her advice?

He sighed. "The City was never designed for children,

86

only to be an effective instrument to destroy the ring. Scientists matter. Women and children come a poor second."

He gazed bleakly into space and she was afraid to interrupt his thoughts. After a while he shrugged and looked kindly at her. "I shall ask you to help me improve matters here. But for the moment there is one more question that puzzles me. What made you decide to come home *now*, if you were so happy as Iriook?"

"Agaguk attacked me. Because of the black snow. It was terrible." She shuddered at the memory. "There was a smell of decay everywhere and the snow turned to slime. And the caribou died. Agaguk said I had done it. He never did believe that I was Iriook the way the others did. He thought I was a bad spirit."

"So he tried to *kill* you?"

"Yes. To frighten me into making the snow go away. It wasn't his fault, you know. It was a reasonable thing for him to do."

"So the fright at being almost killed forced you to remember that you were really Liza? That you belonged to the Techs and not the Ekoes?"

"Yes, sir?"

"Why did he think you were a spirit, and not a Tech? Don't they know about Techs?"

"No. The only real things are the People, the land, the caribou. Anything that doesn't fit into all that is explained as a kind of leaking over from the spirit world. Like when the aeroplanes flew over . . . " She stopped suddenly and stared at Master Bix.

"What is it?"

"The aeroplanes. What were they doing? They couldn't have been looking for me – you would never have wasted the fuel. And I felt something fall. A dew. A dust. Something. And then the black snow began to come. Was it you? It couldn't have been *you* . . . "

Master Bix got abruptly to his feet. "Come. There is something I have to show you."

He led the way along the main hall and down corridor 1E, towards the yeast culture labs, where most of the City's food was grown. She'd worked in there part-time, and very dull it was too. Just rows and rows of vats with gauges which had to be watched, in case anything went wrong, only it never did. Boring.

Master Bix walked rapidly towards the experimental labs at the back. Here nobody but research staff was permitted, for fear of contaminating the cultures. In an ante-room they both put on coveralls that enveloped hands, feet and face. They stood in an ultraviolet sterilizer until the light went out and a farther door opened to admit them to the labs.

Here white-clad men moved quietly about the white-walled white-floored room. The only contrast to the whiteness was the substance that was being skimmed from the surface of small vats, freeze-dried in vacuum ovens, packaged and labelled. It was black, as black as the wet charcoal of a doused fire, as black as the blight on the snow . . .

"It *is* you!" Liza turned to stare at Master Bix. "It's you making the snow black . . . you killing the caribou!"

She felt sick just looking at the slimy stuff. She could not smell it through her protective clothing, but she remembered that it smelt of death. She pushed her way out of the lab and tore off her white overalls. She should have known from the first moment she saw it that it was a Tech thing. It was typical Tech. *Why* hadn't she guessed at once? First the aeroplanes and then the blackness. Damn them. Oh, damn them!

She brushed her hand across her eyes. Not just them. *Her* too. She was a Tech too, wasn't she? Agaguk had wanted to kill her. His reasons were wrong, but his instincts had been dead right.

Master Bix joined her outside the lab. He raised his eyebrows at her face, but said nothing, and when she began to talk he silenced her. "Come."

She obeyed him instinctively and followed him across the width of the City to the Astronomy unit.

"Sit here," he ordered her, and slipped a cassette into a

video unit. A familiar picture showed on the screen.

The Mouth of Paija. She almost said it aloud.

"The ring," Master Bix began to talk in his lecturing voice. "Twenty years ago, before you were born, Liza, the ring was formed. Earth captured a large comet, an infrequent traveller orbiting our sun. It formed a cloud of dust and tectites – glassy particles – around the Earth. These slowly shrank back from the poles to form a deep ring around the equator, a ring like Saturn's, though much denser. The ring cuts about eighty per cent of the sun's energy from reaching the northern and southern latitudes during their respective winters..."

"We learned all this in school," Liza said meekly.

"Bear with me. The first thing that happened was that the winters became longer. More snow fell, and because the summers were much shorter less snow melted. The glaciers grew and began to move down out of the north as they did thirty-five thousand years ago."

"But it's going to be all right, isn't it? John said you were working at finding ways of destroying the ring and pushing back the glaciers."

"Exactly. Unfortunately we have not yet been able to develop a Space Net to skim the dust and tectites off into space and disperse the ring harmlessly. We'll come up with something. Everyone believes that. But can it be done in time, that is the question?"

"In time?" Liza felt a coldness, like the cold of the north, grasp her inside.

"There will come a moment when the balance of heat and cold will tip irrevocably in favour of cold. Once that moment is past there is nothing we can do. Nothing. There will be another Ice Age. It will be the end of most of Europe, the end of North America."

"Even if you destroy the ring?"

"Even so. And the moment is very close, closer than we had expected. Unless we can hold back that thermodynamic clock we are finished."

"The black snow?"

"Yes. Remember that black absorbs heat, while white, particularly if it is a shiny white, reflects it. Once an Ice Age is initiated it grows very rapidly just because more and more of Earth's surface is covered with ice and snow which reflects the sun's energy instead of absorbing it. We must reverse that trend. We must increase the amount of energy that we can absorb from the sun during the short time that it is not hidden behind the ring."

"So you invented the black snow?"

"Yes. It's a mould, the sort of thing we tend to find contaminating our cultures – normally a nuisance. It multiplies furiously, and initially seems to thrive on nothing but air, heat and water. This is our test year. The spores have been scattered over thousands of hectares of northland and allowed to grow naturally. And it works! It works as powdered charcoal or soot never could, because it grows and spreads by itself. It's the answer."

"But next winter it'll snow again and cover it all up."

"That's all right. Next spring we'll seed again, completely this time, the whole of the northland right up to and over the ice sheet. We'll seed the black spores every summer until we've designed a Space Net to rid us of the ring for ever. It's like sandbags holding back a river in flood. It doesn't solve the question of why the river floods and how it can be stopped. But it saves people from drowning in the meantime."

"It won't save all the people. Not the Ekoes."

"Liza, I'm talking about the population of the northern hemisphere. How do you suppose that weighs up against the Ekoes? How many are there – fifty, a hundred, a thousand?"

Liza shook her head. "I don't know. There were thirteen in *our* family. They spoke of others, but I never met them. Don't *you* know all about them, sir?"

"My dear girl, you already know much more than we do. They live off the land. They have no permanent settlement. They don't register their births and deaths. They are on no official census. Technically, they simply don't exist."

90

"But they *do*! Only they won't much longer. If you go on poisoning the caribou they'll die, all of them. And you'll have killed them."

I'll have killed them too, she thought, and buried her face in her hands.

"What's the matter?"

"I persuaded Namoonie to bring me here by promising I'd find a way of getting rid of the black snow. But it was a lie, just a lie to get me away from Agaguk. I didn't know that the Techs, that *we*, were responsible."

"I thought he didn't understand about the Tech culture, about the City?"

"He doesn't. He thought it was a spirit place. I said I'd get the cure from the spirits."

"And believing it was a spirit place he still brought you here? What a brave young man!"

Liza blushed and smiled. "Yes, he is, isn't he?"

"It's most fortunate that we have him here. I believe that our best plan would be for Namoonie to help us pick up his group of Ekoes by plane, and hopefully tell us where we can find the others. They can live in the City until we've managed to destroy the ring. Once their environment returns to normal they can go back – if they should still wish to."

His tone of voice made it clear that he didn't believe that they would want to, after savouring the life of the City.

He is a very wise man, Liza thought. Perhaps the wisest man in the country. He must know what's best. But . . . how will the People survive without the caribou? And the caribou *will* die. They couldn't airlift the caribou out of the north-land. Even if they could they would probably just go back, following their own relentless instincts.

"I don't think Namoonie is going to understand that you've got to do it, that it's for the best."

"It'll be your job to make that clear, Liza. I will start organizing the pick-up immediately. You can explain what we need him to do in the morning."

Oh, Namoonie, Liza thought. When you know that I am

truly Tech, and you understand what the Techs have done, will you listen to me?

"Go back to bed." Master Bix patted her shoulder. "Stop worrying. We will take care of your friends."

She slept badly, in her cold bed in the hospital, and it seemed to her that she had hardly closed her eyes before her shoulder was being shaken. The morning lights had not been turned on. There was only the glow of the emergency lights. It must be very early.

"Wake up, Liza. Wake up!"

She groaned. "Huh?"

"You have to wake up. The Eko boy has escaped."

"What?" She jolted awake and sat up, staring through her tangled hair.

"He's gone all right. Hit the guard with a chair and made off. You're wanted."

Liza threw on her uniform with shaking hands, and scrambled into her sandals. Lord, wrong feet. Try again ... Namoonie gone? Where?

Within three minutes she was standing breathlessly in Master Bix's office. The guard sat nursing his head. The broken chair lay in the chaos of overturned files.

"Has he left the City?" Liza burst out without even pausing for a sketchy greeting.

"We think not. The Summer Door was locked soon after sunset."

"But the Winter Door. It would be open, wouldn't it? I came that way. He saw me. He'll remember."

"He wouldn't find it in a million years. This place must seem like a maze to him." His voice sounded condescending.

Liza flushed angrily. "Namoonie led me back to the place where he first found me, where the sled was dropped off, with no trouble at all. It was ten months later. There were no signs, no tracks, just bare land. But he did it. Finding his way out of the City will be simple."

"I hope you're wrong."

"So do I. If he leaves now he'll starve. We finished the meat."

Master Bix shuddered. "So unpleasant. We must get them accustomed to more civilized food."

"I ate meat too, all the time I lived with them."

"I know. I smelt you."

"And drank blood too!" Why did she say that? Did she want to shock him? To ally herself with the People? She blushed at his expression and changed the subject. "Shouldn't we be looking for Namoonie?"

"It's being done. The guards are systematically searching the City. It shouldn't take long, since almost everyone is still in bed..."

A buzz interrupted his words. He lifted the phone. As soon as he replaced it it buzzed again.

Liza waited tensely. Five buzzes. One from each floor and from the basement. Did she want him to be found? Or to get away? Only how would he survive without any food but fish?

Master Bix put down the phone for the last time. "Well, you were right. He has got away, and well equipped too. Supplies are missing."

She said nothing, but she couldn't help the smile widening across her face.

"How far is his home?"

"They don't have a special home. Everywhere is..."

Master Bix sighed impatiently. "Back to wherever you left the others, then?"

"I don't know. We walked for nearly a moon – a month, I mean."

"Direction?"

"We came mostly south. East for a little while and then south."

"Well, that shouldn't be too much of a problem. He can't have got far. We'll get out a helicopter. You'd better go along too."

Liza struggled with her own very mixed up feelings. "Master Bix, *don't*. Please let him go."

"Let him go? Why? The caribou are dying, and they can't live without them. You said that yourself. I don't understand. I thought you cared for the boy."

"I do. That's why. I mean, I understand him. He doesn't belong in the City. It's like a prison. He hates it already, and the others will hate it too. They have to be free."

"Didn't you hate the conditions of life with the Ekoes? Weren't you afraid at first?"

"Y ... yes."

"But you grew to love it so much that you were able to forget your Tech background, your family, even your own name."

"Yes, but..." Liza didn't have the words to argue with a man as clever as Master Bix. How could she explain to him that perhaps you might set a tame bird free and teach it to survive, but that to cage a free bird and train it to be content with its prison was wrong. Anyway, who was she to tell him, but a girl and the lowest among the low, while he was Master Bix.

"Please let him go," she begged again.

It was just as if she hadn't spoken. "Report to the Winter Door. There'll be a helicopter ready. Shocking waste of fuel. I wish it hadn't happened." He nodded dismissal and picked up the phone again.

I could hide, she thought. Just not go. But what would be the point? They'd send out the helicopter anyway. And Namoonie would be terrified. At least she could help him...

When she reached the Winter Door the helicopter had already been hauled up from the storage area and its blade was being fixed into the 'open' position. There were two men aboard, construction men, obviously picked for their size and weight. Charles Weyburn was the pilot. He was nice. Was there any chance that she could persuade him to let Namoonie escape? No, that was crazy. Without smiling she took her place beside him and fastened her safety belt.

I can't stop him, she thought angrily, but I'm certainly not going to help.

So when Charles asked her: "Which direction will he be going?" she sat with her lips in a tight line, staring straight ahead as if she hadn't heard.

Charles sighed. "Oh, Liza! He left a little over an hour ago. At a speed of nine kilometres an hour he hasn't got far. We'll only need to search a hundred square kilometres or so. How long do you think it's going to take us to cover that? It's nothing! Give us some help and save time and fuel, there's a good girl."

Liza shrugged and wouldn't look at him. Charles switched on, juggled the controls. They lifted and swooped above the City hill. "We'll do a spiral search north westerly," he spoke over his shoulder to the heavyweights in the back. "Keep your eyes open for any movement. He shouldn't be too hard to spot. There's no place to hide in this country."

Liza hid a smile. The sun had just risen and was sending long shadows rippling across the land. Summer was at its peak. The grass was high. In the small creeks that furrowed the land were occasional clumps of scrub willow. An empty land, but there were still many hiding places, if a person only understood that he should hide.

Would Namoonie realise that the Techs *were* human, that they were searching for him with only human eyes, that if he remained still and hidden they would never see him. Stay still, Namoonie, she told him silently. In the grass. Beneath the willows. In the shadow of a creek. Wherever you are, stay still. We are not spirits. We cannot see through things. We cannot pierce shadows. Stay still.

At the extreme edge of her vision she caught a small flicker of movement. She willed her head not to turn towards it, her hands to remain relaxed in her lap. The others saw nothing. A few minutes later, when they passed directly above the place where she had seen the movement, she saw nothing either. The pattern continued, a spiral slowly unwinding from the City north west until it reached a distance of ten kilometres.

"I'll take a couple more turns," Charles said half to himself. "But I don't see how he could have got this far over that rough terrain. Don't see how we could have missed him either."

Liza stared straight ahead, ignoring his look. She held her triumph inside her, careful that none of it should spill over where it might be seen.

"Okay, boys, we'll head back." Charles' voice was briskly matter-of-fact. She couldn't tell if he was disappointed at their failure. Perhaps he just didn't care, one way or the other. Perhaps to him it was just a job, like spraying poisonous spores over the land.

As soon as the helicopter landed, Liza jumped out and ran through the Winter Door and down the tunnel. She laughed out loud. Namoonie had beaten the City. He was smarter than all the Techs put together. Good for Namoonie!

But ... Oh, I'll never see you again, she thought. And suddenly felt as cold and empty as the barren lands when the first winds of winter begin to blow across them.

9

"I'm glad Namoonie got away!" Liza said defiantly, and at least part of her meant it. "He didn't belong in the City, you could see that. His place is out there." She waved her hand vaguely. "Free."

"But what a price to have to pay for freedom," Master Bix spoke softly. "Hunger. Cold. Constant discomfort. And above all, no advancement. Do you understand, Liza? The Ekoes have done a splendid job of adapting to an almost impossible environment. But in doing so they have had to turn their backs on the goals that Man has spent thousands of years reaching toward. Science. Literature. The arts..."

"Are we any better off, sir? I mean, there's no art in the City. No music except for what the old ones remember. And look at what *we've* given up, hiding underground. It's so beautiful outside, sir, sleeping under the stars. Hearing the earth wake up in the springtime. Being close to it..."

"Romantic twaddle!" One of the listening scientists broke in. Liza had almost forgotten them, sitting around the table in the conference room. "Arthritis and skin diseases and malnutrition. That's what your romantic outdoor life leads to."

Master Bix raised an admonishing hand and the man subsided grumpily. "As for art and music, we hold the memory of what has been accomplished in the past as most precious; and more will be done in the future. But now we in the north have no time. That, for the moment, is *our* sacrifice, in order to hold back the ice. Our way of life is purposeful. The Ekoes' is not. It is a dead end, Liza. Can't you see that?"

She shook her head stubbornly, remembering the love of Kidlak and Nawpachee, of the children. How could that sort of loving kindness be a 'dead end'?

Master Bix sighed. "I hoped that together we might be able to persuade you to help us find Namoonie after all, make him lead us to the others and warn them of the danger of the snow mould."

"The danger? They *know* the danger, you didn't. I had to tell you what the black snow was doing to the caribou. But why are you talking? You're not going to go ahead with it now you know, are you? You can't!"

There was silence. Liza stared wildly round at the faces of the assembled scientists. Her own father was among them, identically uniformed, his bland face telling her nothing of his thoughts or feelings.

Her own face whitened and then flushed with anger. "You *have* to stop, now that you know. You won't use it again next spring?" She stared at the blank impassive faces. No, not quite impassive. Their eyes would not meet hers. None of them but Master Bix's. She spoke directly to him. "If you go on now, knowing what you do, then it's murder."

"It is only the caribou who get sick when they eat the moss and lichen that the black spores have infected. Only the caribou will die."

"And won't their meat slowly poison the People?"

"Not necessarily. Impurities tend to migrate to the liver and the fatty tissue. If they will just avoid..." Tim Peters' voice trailed off in the face of Liza's scorn.

"Don't you know anything? They'll die without the fat and liver. It's the only way they can get vitamins. And anyway, what is going to happen when the caribou have all died, or so many of them that the People can't find them any more? If the People starve slowly instead of being poisoned, it'll still be murder, and it'll still be your fault."

"And yours too." Master Bix's voice was like a whip. "*You* refused to help us find Namoonie. *You* refused to persuade him to bring his people here. If we are going to talk about blame and how we are to apportion it, then you must bear your share."

Liza went white again. Her father moved abruptly, but was stilled by a sign from Master Bix. The second hand of the clock above the door jerked busily round. It was the only movement in the room.

"Can't you find another mould?" she asked piteously. "One that isn't poisonous?"

"Oh, child, you don't know what you're asking. That one was a freak, a chance accident of nature, a throw of the dice. Once it occurred we realised its possibilities and began to work. It's taken three years," Tim Peters burst out again.

"But we're talking about people's lives. Time can't be as important as lives."

It was as if she had hit a sore spot. They all began to talk at once, each justifying himself in his own way. Master Bix got to his feet with a quick movement that stopped the uproar in midsentence.

"Liza, look at this map," he flipped it across the table to her. "Do you know what it represents?"

"It's a circumpolar map. The north pole in the centre and the northern hemisphere spread out around it."

"Correct. Do you see the blue lines drawn on it? They represent the ice-line at the end of summer for the last ten years. That is, the line above which snow has not melted, so that in the following winter new snow falls on old, each year becoming a little deeper, more compressed, until it turns into glacial ice. Do you understand?"

"Yes, sir." She peered at the map. "The lines are dated."

"Yes. Go on. What else?"

The wavy blue lines looked like the sea breaking on a white shore, closer together the farther back in time you looked. "The last two years, the lines are much farther apart. The snow line is advancing south more rapidly?"

"Much more rapidly. I already told you that it won't be long before it is irreversible. Look at the map, Liza. The whole of North America, much of Europe and Asia. Civilization buried under a mile of ice for thousands of years. Death. Starvation. The end of Man's dreams of a good future. And *we* can halt that."

"You said it was only a sandbag. You've still got to break up the ring."

"It's the breathing space we need. We're near. So near! If we can just hold back those blue lines next summer, the few summers after that. The whole world's resources are being pooled to build the Space Net, to gather up the particles and disperse them safely into space. Meanwhile the world is watching us. Here is where the ice is advancing the most rapidly. Here in western Canada."

"It's the Ekoes' land too. They deserve life as much as the rest of us."

"Tell them so." Master Bix slipped the map among his papers. "Help us find them. Tell them that we'll give them a home until the north is safe again, if they should still wish to return to that way of life."

"And the caribou? Will you give them a home too?"

"Now you're being stupid."

"No, I'm not." Liza felt angry tears spring to her eyes. She was too proud to brush them away in front of these men. She stared through them. "You really haven't listened to what I've said, have you? You don't really care what happens to them. You've no intention of changing your plans. You never did. I was crazy to think that you'd help."

"Only a few people against the billions in the rest of the world, Liza. Against civilization..." Her father spoke for the first time.

"I'm not that thrilled with a civilization that won't count people like Namoonie and his family because they don't wash too often or clip their toenails. Why did you bother calling me here just to make a fool of myself, when you'd no intention of helping..." She choked.

Master Bix spread his white hands delicately. "We felt we at least owed you an explanation. And the offer still holds. Lead us to Namoonie and persuade him to bring his people here. Whatever you may think, we're not murderers."

The tears ran down her cheeks. She didn't care any more. "May I go, please?"

"You may. I'm sorry, Liza ..."

"*Sorry?*"

"Sorry that you won't cooperate with us."

She left the room, shutting the door behind her hard enough for it to be a slam. There was an uncomfortable silence, broken by Liza's father. "I'd like to wash my mouth out."

"It's all in a good cause, David." Tim put a hand on his shoulder. "What about it? Do you think she'll take the bait, Master Bix?"

"As sure as one can be with the psycho-profile of a teenager. They're nothing if not changeable."

"You sure there's no possibility of losing her? My God, Master Bix, if it happened again, I don't know what her mother and I would do..."

"We won't lose her, David. You can be sure of that. There's a directional bug hidden in the vehicle, and a personal mike in her uniform. It was sewn in last night, while she slept."

"It's a stinking thing to do."

"What's the alternative? Scrap the programme? Condemn those innocent people to a slow death?"

"Suppose they still won't come?"

"Then we'll have to be true to our priorities, won't we? Just as we told Liza."

"Yes, but . . . good lord . . ."

"Do we have any other options, gentlemen?"

10

Liza left Master Bix in a blind rage, and stood hesitating outside the door. Right now her shift would be down in Fabrics, working the looms. She looked down at her shaking hands. I can't, she thought. I've got to be away by myself.

The hall was almost empty. Under the shadows of the stairs was the door to the basement. 'Authorized Personnel only'. It was quiet down there, and she'd be alone to straighten out her thinking. The sign didn't bother her. She'd broken more important rules than this and the sky hadn't fallen in.

She glanced around and slipped into the shadows and was through the door before anyone could have noticed. It was cool and dark. And empty, as it had been that other time, when she'd stowed away. Ten months ago, the start of the expedition . . .

I wish I'd never gone, she thought. Now the tears she had held back poured down her face. If I'd never met Namoonie I wouldn't care. When the black snow threatened their way of life I'd never know. I wouldn't hurt like this . . .

But it would still be happening to *them*. You don't make

sense, Liza. They'd be just as dead, whether you knew about it or not. And what about Namoonie? Would you really rather never have known him? Truly..?

Oh, hell! She blew her nose. She did know him, and because of him she felt alive as she'd never felt before. And life would never be the same because of knowing him. And that was all there was to it. So what was she going to do about it?

Where was Namoonie now? He was three days away from the City. Three walking days. She could never catch him up, even if she could pick up his trail, which was doubtful. But suppose she were to take a crawler? Even if he walked at a most prodigious pace she would still be able to catch up with him in five or six hours. Eight at the most. If she were to leave now she should have caught up with him by twilight...

Except that there was no way of finding him. She could be right on his trail and never see him. He was the one who could find his way blindfolded over the barrens. He could find *her* all right. If he wanted to. Would he want to?

Her tears dried up. She sniffed and stuck her jaw out. It's worth a try, she thought. What have I got to lose? If I can only find a crawler fuelled up and ready to go.

She walked purposefully across the wide storage area to the tunnel that led up to the Winter Door. There was a whole row of crawlers, and the two City helicopters, looking like dead insects with their rotor blades dismantled. She stopped beside the crawler that was parked closest to the tunnel. She listened, with her hand on the door frame. Nothing. There was nobody down here.

She climbed in and looked at the back seat. There were sleeping bags. Cans of petrol. Food packages. Everything in order. They must be planning to move out today, maybe even in the next few minutes.

Hurry, then! She turned the ignition key and tentatively pushed her foot on the pedal. The engine roared into violent life. Shhh. Ease off a bit. The gauges flickered. She didn't know what most of them meant, but the one that said 'fuel' stood at 'full'. So far, so good.

There didn't seem to be much to it. She hadn't driven a crawler before, but she knew the theory. That was the acceleration. This one the brake. And this lever moved from 'park' to 'drive'. And that seemed to be that. She hoped she'd never have to go backwards. Could crawlers go backwards? She swallowed. Come on, Liza, what are you waiting for, an audience?

She slid the weathertight door shut. Better to start right now before she scared herself off thinking how crazy her idea was. The engine chugged away comfortably. She moved the lever to 'drive' and put her foot down carefully. The crawler lurched towards the tunnel.

It was dark in there and the engine made an incredible amount of noise. She must be advertising her escape to the whole City. Lights. Where were the lights? She turned switches on and off. The tunnel suddenly sprang into view. With her tongue caught between her teeth she eased her foot down onto the accelerator pedal. The crawler began to climb the steep slope. Past the first open door. The second. The exit was a square of light growing steadily bigger. She switched off the lights. Now she was level with the last door.

As the crawler lurched through the door onto the hillside above the City, heat and light struck her in the face. The sun stood high above the ring to her right. Her eyes squinted and watered. Her way lay in the other direction, to the left. So long as the crawler chased its own shadow across the land she would be moving in the right direction.

She turned the steering wheel carefully, bouncing in her seat as the crawler's wide treads chewed up stones on the slope beneath. Down into the valley behind the City she went, and up the farther slope. All the time there was a feeling of eyes boring into her back. She had a terrible urge to look back over her shoulder to see if indeed anyone had spotted her. She had to force herself to keep her eyes on the way ahead, to avoid big boulders or the particularly bright patches of green which might signal a patch of muskeg deep enough to bog down the crawler.

At last another low hill lay between her and the City and she felt easier. There was a compass mounted above the instrument panel, and she tried to maintain a north-north-westerly course, as far as she could for threading her way between low hills, avoiding boulders and the deeper-looking creeks.

Her ears were still alert for the sounds of pursuit: the grumbling engine of another crawler, the clip-clop of a helicopter. A great shadow swooped overhead and she pulled up, her heart pounding, the sweat running down her neck. But it was only the silent shadow of an eagle. While she watched, it slipped sideways down an air current and hurtled towards the ground, braking at the last terrifying second with wide-arched wings and extended feather-covered legs. Almost without pause it rose again, a small brown animal dangling from its talons.

Liza wiped her face and pushed open the cab window. It was getting awfully hot inside. Why, she was actually shaking!

The air smelled fresh and sweet after the recycled air of the City. It was filled with the sounds of birds and insects and the sound of water.

She sighed and leaned back, and for a moment let the peace wash over her, dissolving away the fear and tension. It was going to be all right. Nobody had noticed the loss of the crawler. Nobody had seen her leave. Somewhere ahead of her, not too far away, was Namoonie. She was going to find him, and then he would take her back to the people. She started to drive again.

The sun vanished in a blood-red welter that flooded the sky almost to the zenith, and tinged the land with an unearthly pink glow. With lights on Liza could have driven all night, but that was not part of her plan.

She stopped and climbed stiffly down. There was a gully

crowded with willows, and she broke off branches and hauled out deadfall from the choked creek until she had a big pile of wood on high ground.

She didn't have the People's skill at firemaking, but she made a large pyramid of sticks, shook a little kerosene onto the wood and tossed in a match. The fire roared into life, its pale flames fading out the sunset colours so that the sky seemed suddenly darker. She pulled out the sleeping bags, and made a comfortable place to sit. Then she opened two of the food kits and laid them out on a flat stone close to the fire.

It's a pity I have no meat to roast, she thought. The scent of meat juices and burning fat would draw a hungry man like magic. But at least the fire was very bright, and up on the hill must be visible for kilometres.

There was nothing else to see but the night shadows folding around her. There was nothing to hear but the crackling of the fire. A man walking in fur boots on dry grass in the middle of the night might as well be invisible, inaudible. A little breeze made her shiver, as if a person were breathing down her neck. But that's all it was – a little breeze.

When her arms were grasped suddenly from behind she gasped, not really a scream, but it was unexpected like that in the dark, even though she'd been waiting for him.

She forced her body to relax. She ran her tongue over her lips and smiled, so that the smile would be in her voice, talking in the dark to the one she could not see.

"Greetings, Namoonie. I have prepared food after your journey." She used the familiar phrases that Kidlak or Nawpachee would have used. The hard hands on her arms relaxed their grip just a little.

"You are alone?" His breath was warm against the back of her neck.

"You must know that I am. Have you not been watching me since you saw my fire, soon after the sun began to fade?" She spoke pertly, and he chuckled, let go her arms and sat down beside her on the sleeping bags.

She picked up one of the plastic trays. "Eat then."

He looked at it. "Spirit food!"

She could not see his face. It was shadowed, as the flames moved through the fire, with moving shadows. "It is real food, Namoonie. It is as good for you as meat. We have lived on it for as long as I can remember, and we are all very healthy." She picked a protein-filled bun off her tray and bit into it. "It's very good," she mumbled. "Try it, Namoonie."

"It will not turn me into a spirit?"

"It will not."

He paused. She saw his hand reach out for the food and she relaxed. They ate in silence and washed down the food with the sweet peat-brown water that ran down the hill towards the creek.

"Why did you come back? I thought you did not care. You ran into the hillside, left me for the spirit people to take as if there was nothing between us, as if our time together had no meaning."

"I'm sorry." The words were inadequate, but Liza did not know what else to say. She clasped her hands together, twisting the fingers around each other. "I felt . . . muddled. I wanted to get back into the City, to my own people, and you were stopping me. So I ran. I thought you would follow me through the Winter Door. I didn't understand until afterwards what it must have seemed like to you – as if the earth had swallowed me up."

"I thought the spirits had taken you. I thought they would also reach out for me, and I was afraid. I hid. I too am ashamed."

"You've got nothing to be ashamed of, Namoonie. You were wonderfully brave! You could have gone back, but you stayed . . ."

"And let them catch me as if I were a child!"

"You couldn't have stopped them. They had medicine to make you sleep. They would never have caught you otherwise. And look how you escaped them!"

He chuckled cheerfully and bit into his food. "Ayee! That will be a story to tell! I escaped from the Hill, but they sent a

106

thing like a bird after me, an eagle that hovered, with a terrible noise like this..." He waved his arms in a circle and imitated a helicopter motor so well that Liza began to laugh.

"I thought they would see me, but I hid in a patch of willows, and though the metal eagle passed straight over my head it never saw me. So I began to think that the creatures of the spirit world were not so clever after all. Why are you laughing, Iriook?"

"Because you're funny, and it's so good to see you again. And because *I* was in that metal eagle, and I saw you, just before you hid."

"But you did not tell them? They went away."

"Of course I didn't! What do you take me for? We are friends, aren't we? They made me go on the search, but I wouldn't help them find you."

"Friends? I thought we were more than that, Iriook. Has that too changed?"

Liza felt a fluttering inside her and it was difficult to breathe. She felt warm all over. "I don't know, Namoonie." She tried to keep her voice steady, as if she wasn't having all these strange feelings, but it shook a little in spite of her efforts. "There are other things more important now, things that we must talk about."

"You didn't come back because of us?"

"Yes. No. Not only in the way you mean. Namoonie, you have got to warn the People, not just the family, but all the People, about the black snow. It's very bad, and, oh Namoonie, *my* people made it – the City Techs. Next spring they plan to spread it over the whole land."

"But it will kill the caribou."

"I know. *They* know."

"The caribou have been here always. The Great Spirit put the caribou on the land so that the People would always have shelter and food and clothing."

"I know, Namoonie."

"Without the caribou my People are dead!"

"That's what I told them." Liza burst into tears.

107

"Then surely they will stop."

"They won't. That's why I came back. Oh, Namoonie, I'm so sorry. I tried and tried to make them understand. They're not wicked. They're not trying to kill you, you have to see that. The blackness is a way of pushing back the ice that is creeping down out of the north. Once the ice covers the whole land, that will be the end of your people and mine as well, the end of us all."

"I do not see that. I have heard that the ice is greater every year, but it is not so much greater that anything bad will happen in our lifetimes."

"It will later on. We have to think of the future."

"Why?"

"Because if we don't there won't *be* any future."

"Even if it becomes colder I do not see why we cannot go on the way we have. Cannot your people learn to live as we do. Why do you fight the country? Can you not accept it and bend to it the way one bends before the wind?"

"It's not possible. We're such a different kind of people. And..." She understood at last what Master Bix had tried to tell her, though then she had been too angry to listen to him. How could she tell Namoonie that existing from one caribou hunt to the next, always on the move, one's whole energy taken up in living and eating, that Man could not advance that way? There had to be time over for asking questions about the Universe, for trying to find answers...

"You have songs and stories to remind you of the past of the People, Namoonie. We have so many memories and so much learning that it has filled thousands of books. If the ice comes we will lose all that has been learned since Man came out of the caves after the last ice."

"If you have so much learning can you not stop the ice?"

"Yes! But not quite yet. Just a few more years. If we can only hold the ice for a little while with the black snow."

"Why did you follow me to tell me this? What is your reason? Is it a courtesy to give us time to learn how to die? To make the right songs and dances? You should not have been concerned. The People already know how to die."

"But I don't want you to. You don't have to." Liza's voice choked with tears, and she swallowed them and struggled on. Why *had* she come? There was nothing one girl could do. "It's not fair, Namoonie. You've got as much right to life as our people. But the Techs say that if there are only thirteen of you against the billions in the rest of the world, you just don't count."

"There are more than thirteen of us. There are tens of tens."

"Where? I've never seen anyone else."

"All across the land. We do not live together because there is so little wood. If we live more than two or three days apart from each other, then there is enough wood for all."

"Do you ever meet?"

"Of course. We are the People! At the last kill before the caribou go back to the land of the sun for the winter we come together. We exchange songs and stories. Many many people, tens of tens. Is that as many as *your* people?"

"No, Namoonie." Liza sighed. "It is nothing like as many. But perhaps it will be enough, if we all get together and tell the Techs that they have to stop."

"Will they listen?"

"I don't know. But I honestly can't think of anything else to do."

Namoonie was silent. Together they sat by the dying fire. The sky blazed with stars, but already in the east a pale pre-dawn light strengthened. The land stretched emptily away in every direction, unyielding, eternal. It seemed to Liza that it rejected her and her kind utterly. She shivered.

"What is it?" Namoonie put his arm around her.

"I don't know. Cold. Tired perhaps." She would have added – lonely, but now that his arm was around her it made a lie out of the word.

"You have travelled far and fast, Iriook. You must give your soul time to catch up. Sleep now. In the morning we will begin the journey to meet the People."

11

The skin drum throbbed. The voices chanted in a rhythm that seemed to Liza to match the beating of her own heart. The smoke rose thickly and flattened in a sudden north-westerly wind that chased away the mosquitoes. She crouched in her place in the great circle between Kidlak and Namoonie, her hands on her knees, her eyes on the figure of the man in the centre of the circle.

He seemed as old as the northland itself. His face cracked into a thousand wrinkles like sun-dried mud. His eyes were almost invisible in the creases of his eyelids. His swollen knuckles beat the skin drum and caused the small carved shapes on its surface to move and jump about as if they had a life of their own. From time to time he peered at the carvings, as if to mark their position on the painted skin. Then his voice would rise again, and he would beat the skin with renewed vigour.

Like a heartbeat, Liza thought again, a heart beating faster and faster as if one had been running. She could feel her own pulse race and her breathing quicken to keep up with the imperative beat of the drum. When at last the pounding stopped with shocking suddenness, it felt as if her heart too had stopped. She felt dizzy and faint.

In the silence the old man bounded from the centre of the circle and stood directly in front of her. She gasped and flinched. One wrinkled brown hand pointed at her. The other still held the drum. She could see that the designs on its surface had been newly painted over other designs that had long faded. They were in a brownish red that was surely blood.

"Who are you?" the old man challenged.

The sudden gasp had cleared her head of the heavy hypnotic trance that the monotonous drum beat had induced. She answered readily. "My name is Liza and I am a Tech

110

from the City. But to the family of Kidlak and Agaguk I am Iriook, who was lost in the snows of three winters ago."

"How can a person be two people at once?"

Liza thought rapidly. She had to make them believe her, or they would not listen to her message and they could die. How could she explain? Not in psychological terms, the way Techs would. She looked at little Soo and Ashoona, and from their knowledge drew what she needed.

"When the ptarmigan lays an egg, it is the promise of another ptarmigan inside the shell, is it not?"

She looked around the circle, trying to draw them to her in friendship. There were encouraging nods from her own family, impassive stares from the strangers.

"But to the child gathering eggs in springtime, the egg is the promise of good food today, not the promise of a ptarmigan in a moon. Yet is one way of looking at the egg wrong and the other right?"

There was a pause. "They are both right," a voice stated from across the circle, and there was a general movement, a nodding agreement.

Liza drew a shaky breath. "So it is possible for a person to be two things at the same time. I am Liza, a Tech, when I am in the City. With you I am Iriook."

"Tell me truly. Are you the same Iriook who was lost?" The old man thrust his wrinkled face close to hers. She could smell smoke and fat and dried blood.

"No, I am not," she answered boldly. Agaguk let out his breath in a triumphant "Hah!" Sadly Liza felt Kidlak's arm draw back from her. She turned and spoke directly to the mother of Iriook. "I am like the baby caribou whose mother dies. He is suckled by another who has lost her young one. I am not part of her flesh, and yet I do belong, through love and need."

She could see the tears glint in the woman's eyes, and, though Kidlak did not speak, her arm was once again warm against Liza's side.

The old man grunted and drew back. "You have spoken

truly. It is good that you have done so, for that is the message that the sacred drum told me. Now you must explain to us why, after you took Iriook's place in her mother's heart, you left. And, having left, why you came back again from a world where you do not have to hunt for food, where you sleep warm, where it is light whenever you choose it to be, even in the middle of winter..."

"Ayeee!" A whisper of amazement ran around the circle.

"It is indeed a wondrous place," Liza answered slowly, speaking in the formal manner of the old man. "And it is everything that you have said. But I found something here, out in the barrens, under the stars, that is missing in the City. I found love. It is because of this love that I have come back. Because of Kidlak. Because of Ottochie and Kumwartok and Ashoona. Because of Ruthee and Soo. Because of Namoonie."

Liza's voice shook and she paused for a moment, willing herself into control, so that she could keep the same singsong storytelling mode of the shaman's. "I have come back because I loved you, and to warn you of the danger of the black snow. I have come to tell you that unless you will fight for it, your way of life will come to an end."

"Fight against spirits?" One of the strangers spoke up. "A man would be crazy to fight spirits."

"The Techs are not spirits. Truly, they are men just as you are. And the City is a real place, not a spirit one. It is as real as a snow house or a tent."

"How can we fight metal birds and blackness that falls from the sky?"

"These things are strange to you because you are not accustomed to them. You have the skills to live in the barrens, to build snow houses, to hunt caribou without guns. You have the skills to bend to Nature and learn her ways. We, the Techs, have none of these skills. Techs have learned to survive by making machines to fight the cold instead of adapting to it, to make food instead of hunting for it. It is a different way. It is not better than yours or worse. Only different. But because of their kind of skill they are able to work on a very big thing that you could never do, a big machine that will take away the badness that Wolverine did in the beginning time."

She pointed to the southern sky. The summer night was beginning. The Mouth of Paija was not visible, but you could see where it was by the black curve in the sky where no stars shone. There was a wordless gasp from the listening circle. The old man waddled across to her and grasped her wrist. How old he is, she thought. His fingers are like dry birds' bones. Later she saw the bruises that they left on her arm.

" Now you lie! Or the Techs are indeed spirits, the most powerful of tornrait, more powerful than ... to undo the mischief of Wolverine? It is not possible!"

"It is and I do not lie." She stared back at the shaman, not impudently but firmly, so that he could see into her eyes. "For men to fly might seem an impossible magic to you, but it is not. Men have flown in aeroplanes for years. If the older of you think back you will remember metal birds flown by men going across the barren lands in the long-ago time before Wolverine made the mischief."

The shaman grunted and released her wrist. "Continue."

She rubbed her arm and concentrated on getting the right words together. "When the Mouth of Paija is once again closed as it was in the beginning times, then once more the sun will shine all year round, except in the month of winter darkness. Then the land will grow warmer. There will be less snow and more food for the caribou. And the ice will go back into the north where it belongs."

A sigh ran round the circle.

"That would be a very great magic," the shaman said. "If indeed it were possible. We have danced and sung the most powerful songs we know, to ask Paija to close her mouth and stop eating up the sun, but Paija has never listened."

"It will take a different kind of magic – Tech magic – to make it happen. And it will take a long time. Two, three winters. Maybe more."

"Each winter is a little colder and longer. When the wind

blows off the ice it freezes the flesh of my children. It is hard when their stomachs are empty and the fat has all been eaten," a woman suddenly spoke up.

"You speak the truth," Liza acknowledged politely. "The Techs have thought of a way of holding back the cold until they can make the big magic."

"Ah!"

"Let them use it!"

"That is good!"

Liza looked around the circle. All eyes were on her. She took a deep breath. "It is the black snow," she admitted.

The exclamations of praise changed to an angry muttering that rose in intensity like the sound before a storm when the first snow whips along the frozen surface of the land. She raised her voice. "It is necessary for all the people of the world."

"It will kill the caribou. Already the land is becoming poisoned. How can we live without the caribou?"

"You cannot. That is why I am here. Will you all come and talk to the Techs and tell them not to do this thing? Tell them that they are killing *you*."

In the silence that followed her words the shaman spoke again. "I see no journey in the future of my people," he said. "Tell me truly, when you lived in the place of the Techs did you not ask them to stop the black snow?"

"Of course I did."

"Did you tell them about the caribou? Did you tell them that without the caribou we would die?"

"Yes, of course I did," Liza shouted. "But they wouldn't listen. They said that when it came to balancing a very few people against everyone else in the world, you were too few to matter."

"I see no journey in the future of my people," the old man said again. "If the Techs will not listen to one of their own, why would they choose to listen to us?"

"There is another way," Liza suggested. "Come back to the City with me. They will give you a home until Paija's

114

mouth is closed and the northland is clean and safe again. Truly, you are welcome."

"What about the caribou? Is the grazing good inside the Hill? Will they mate there and produce young?"

"Of course not." Liza was stung by his tone. Then she remembered that she had said just the same thing to Master Bix. "I am sorry. No, the caribou would have to look after themselves. They might adapt and survive, you know. Animals do sometimes." She didn't really believe it.

Neither did the shaman. "They are dying now. You can promise nothing better than more deaths. I see that in your face. Without the caribou we *have* no life. They are our father and mother."

"Please don't say 'No' right away. Think about it. You would be comfortable in the City. No need to be hungry in winter or suffer from spring weakness because of lack of fat. No need for babies to die. We have doctors who are wise enough to cure almost everything."

"Can they cure what ails a people when they have lost their pride? No, we will not leave."

"Then you'll die too and that will be the end of you for sure. Come to the City. When it's all over and the north is safe we'll work something out. Maybe we can give you food until you have resettled. Perhaps we could bring back the caribou. There must be herds in zoos somewhere ... down in the south..."

The shaman looked around the circle. The faces stared back, sullen, impassive. He picked up the sacred drum and began to beat upon it, so that the carvings jumped. He moved slowly around the circle, looking into each face. Then he began to chant.

"We are the caribou. Kill the caribou and you kill us. We are the land. Kill the land and you kill us. You have given your message, oh girl with two names. Go back to the Techs and tell them what the People of the north say to them."

Liza looked around the circle, at the faces of those she loved, at the faces of those who were still strangers to her, at

Agaguk who had seen from the first that she was nothing but trouble. I won't give up, she thought, and in a clear cold moment knew what she must do.

She stood up and walked into the circle, so that she and the shaman faced each other. "I will not go back to the City and live among murderers," she said. "I am Iriook, daughter of Kidlak and Agaguk, and if they will have me back I will live with them and with the People for ever."

– Until we die, she thought, and her stomach knotted at the thought of the hard winter ahead, and of the next summer with stinking black snow sliming the lichen and the grass and with the swollen bodies of young caribou, their dead legs stiff towards the sky.

"I will stay with the People," she said again, and this time her voice rang out strongly.

"It is good," The old man nodded. "In truth Iriook has returned to the People. Liza is dead and the gate to the spirit world under the Hill is closed for ever."

12

Liza lay sleepless under the stars, the children tumbled warmly about her like puppies. Had she made the right choice? What else could she have done?

Maybe the Techs would think twice about letting one of their own kind die of starvation. But then she had to remember that they had not searched for her when she was missing before – not because she was without worth, but because when they struck a balance between the amount of precious fuel that would be wasted on a search against the value of *one* life, then the need of the whole community for the fuel tipped the balance.

She sighed and turned on the hard ground. Mother and Father seemed as far away and remote as the stars. John even farther . . . John and Win. If she had not yearned to be free she would have stayed in the City and married him. What would her life have been like? Would it have been as cool and efficient as that of her parents? Could she have made it a good life? But she had made her choice ten months before, though she had not known then that she was making any choice at all. It was over now, and she had cut herself off from her beginnings.

But she was not alone. It was good to feel the warmth of Soo's body against her chest. She put her arm around the little girl and held her close. Eventually she slept.

Beyond the gentle rise where the People had gathered and where they now lay asleep, the crawler stood that had brought Liza from the City. From inside the cab a steady stream of signals poured silently out into the night. One of the dogs woke and whined uneasily. One or two of the People heard the whining dog in their sleep, and stirred and dreamed, but no one woke.

The sun was fully up and the blue sky blazed down over the northland when the People woke at last, woke and stretched and sat up, to find themselves surrounded by a silent army of blue-uniformed Techs.

Anger darkened Agaguk's face. "Spirit woman! You brought them. You left open the door of the spirit world and led them here to our secret meeting place. Now I am surely going to kill you!"

It took four of the People to hold him back.

"I didn't bring them. Truly I did not. I don't know how they found this place." Liza shrank back from the wild face of Agaguk, his summer tunic blood-smeared from the hunt, his hair tangled, his eyes slit against the sun. Beyond him she could see the Techs, smooth-faced, clean-cut, clone-like figures in their identical uniforms.

– What am I to do? she thought. I belong to neither of these people, and both of them hate me, for all the wrong reasons.

117

Except Namoonie. She had forgotten Namoonie, who moved forward between her and Agaguk.

"Iriook did not bring these men. You forget that I was with her. They must have followed the tracks of the sled-without-dogs."

"To be able to follow so fast and at night? The girl has bewitched you, Namoonie. I tell you all, she has betrayed us!" Agaguk snarled.

"That is not so!" A familiar figure with a wispy beard stepped from the enclosing circle of Techs. Master Bix! "Liza, it is we who trapped you. I am sorry, but it was necessary. We left the crawler by the Winter Door for you to take, in the hope that you would find your friend and that he would lead you – and us – to his people. There is a homing device on board. We had but to follow it."

Liza stared. "You used me? You made me betray my friends? Oh, Master Bix, how could you...!"

"I had to have a chance to talk to the Ekoes myself, and this was the fastest way. That must be my excuse and my apology."

"They don't want to talk to you. They're afraid of you. Can't you see that?"

"But we've done nothing to hurt them, until the black snow..."

"That's got nothing to do with it. After all, we've always been afraid of Ekoes and they've done less harm to us."

Master Bix stared. "Afraid of Ekoes?"

"Surely you hear the stories the women tell the children in the nurseries? Be good or an Eko will get you. Ekoes will eat people if they should be foolish enough to be out alone after ringset. They live under the snow and can talk to animals..."

"Superstitious twaddle!" Master Bix laughed.

"And yet..." Liza hesitated. "In a way it's close to the truth, but *bent*, you know. Ask your men what they feel about Ekoes, even now, standing around them with stun-guns. Jusk ask."

Master Bix stared around the circle of his men. The answer was clear on their faces, fearful, ashamed, their guns on the huddle of fur-clad people as if they were strange and dangerous animals.

"Well, bless my soul!" Master Bix exclaimed. "And why do the Ekoes hide from us when we explore the ice fields? Old wives' tales too?"

"They believe that you are all spirits living under the ground, and they are afraid that you will make them live under the ground too."

"Which is just what I *do* want. I have come to beg these people to live in the City until we have destroyed the ring."

"It is true what the girl said?" The shaman stepped forward. How strange he looked standing beside Master Bix, Liza thought. Yet he had his own dignity, his own power. "Is it true that you are stronger than Paija, that you speak of destroying the Mouth of Paija?" He pointed south, to the dark bow that smudged the sky.

Liza held her breath. With the wrong words Master Bix could start a riot of People, angry at his blasphemy. But Master Bix had not become Chief of the City without learning what was in people's minds.

"We are as human as you are," he said, looking from the old furrowed face of the shaman to the mad anger of Agaguk. "But our memories are longer so we have more knowledge. What is to you the Mouth of Paija we know to be nothing more than comet dust, circling the earth like a belt. It came out of the heavens and it can be sent back to the heavens. We have nothing to do with Paija, one way or the other."

Agaguk grunted, but the old man nodded his head as though satisfied.

In the silence that followed, Namoonie spoke. "I have been inside your City, and I have ridden in the sled-without-dogs, and so I believe that you can do what you say. But I do not understand, if you are so wise, why you made the black snow. Surely you must have known that it would kill the caribou, and that without the caribou we would die?"

"We did not think about it at all. Our only intention was to melt the snow and hold back the icefield."

"If you have power over the ice you *must* be spirits..."

"Nonsense. It is simply a matter of thermodynamics . . ." Master Bix broke off, shook his head and started again. "The black snow has power to attract the sun. It is the sun that will melt the icefield, not us."

"And if you do not?"

"The ice will cover the land, above the highest mountain."

"Where will the caribou go then?"

"South. Until they reach the places where there are many cities. Then they will die."

"You are telling us that the caribou will die anyway, whether from the black snow or from the great ice?"

"Yes."

Liza interrupted, angry at the way in which Master Bix had woven a net of despair about the People. "It does not have to be that way! Something could be found to turn the snow black that would not poison the caribou. It could!"

"Impossible, dear child. The cost in man-hours and energy. We just could not risk so much on the slender chance of finding something as effective."

"So you will condemn the People to death! Don't they count in your balance of profit and loss? Don't they count at all?"

There was a muttering among the ring of Techs, and a couple of them moved threateningly towards her. Master Bix held up a slender white hand. "She is right. Let her alone. Child, do you think I like what I must do? That I enjoy the choice I must make? At times like this I wish I were the lowest Tech in the yeast lab."

"Someone would have to make these choices, whether it were you or another," she challenged him. She stared straight into his face. She had never dared to do that before. His grey eyes were deeply set. They looked back at her, tired and full of a sadness that came from knowing too much, from being responsible for too much, for making decisions of life and death.

Quite suddenly Liza wanted to put her arms around him,

just as if he were one of the children. But of course she couldn't do that. He was Master Bix. Nor could she take his burden from him. It was his. And if what she said made it harder to bear, that must be so too. The life of the People was at stake.

"You must search for another mould this winter, one that will not poison the land and the caribou. It exists. It must exist. I believe you'll find it, if you'll only try. I'll be waiting to see what your aeroplanes bring at ringrise next year."

"Nonsense! You'll be back in the City where you belong."

She shook her head. "I've already made my choice, Master Bix. I'm staying with the People, to remind you of our existence, out here on the barrens. The City is so comfortable in winter when the windows are shuttered that you might forget about us. But perhaps it will be a little easier to remember when you know that I am with the People, hungry when they are hungry, cold when they are cold. Tell my father that. Perhaps he will look a little harder for an answer. Tell him we will be waiting to see what he sends us at ringrise."

"I could force you to come with us."

"I don't believe you would do that. I trust you, Master Bix. And I trust you to find an answer. Something better."

"Suppose we fail, will you come back then?"

"I belong to the People now. Whatever happens."

By evening only Namoonie's and Iriook's family remained, camped on a low rise from which they could see the empty tundra in every direction. Except for the witness of the ground, torn up by many crawler treads, it might all have been a dream.

Namoonie took Iriook in his arms. "You could have gone back."

"I know."

"But you stayed with us. Why?"

"You're family. I belong."

121

"Then we had better be married, as our mothers planned long ago. We will share this winter, whatever next spring will bring."

Liza/Iriook felt a warmth grow inside her. She felt as if she were finally breaking out of a chrysalis to become whatever she was destined to be from the beginning.

"That is a good idea," she said calmly. "As for ringrise, I am not afraid. I believe that something good will come. And if it does not, well, we will still enjoy the *now*, and not spoil it by being afraid."